a collection of...
Odds & Ends

DANNEY CLARK

DanScribe
Publishing

a collection of...
Odds & Ends

Copyright © 2019 by Danney Clark

ISBN: 9781070283364

Imprint: Independently published

All Rights Reserved

www.danscribepublishing.com

The persons and events portrayed in this work of fiction
are the creations of the author, and any resemblance
to persons living or dead is purely coincidental.

Printed in the United States of America

Dedication

God's perfect plan includes *memory*. Memory is God's way of allowing us to relive events in our lives. We learn and grow from our mistakes, our poor choices, and take joy and inspiration from those which were right and in which we can be proud as we relive them.

This collection of *Odds & Ends* are those things He has brought to mind and which I chose to share with my readers. Praise be to God for allowing me to share them.

Table of Contents

Hopper

"Here, let me help you with that," she heard as she struggled to get the last of her groceries into the cart at Winco. Her 20lb bag of potatoes had placed a noticeable strain on her.

She looked up into the blue eyes of a tall young man smiling down on her, who was balanced precariously on his single remaining leg. A thick shock of sandy blond hair gave him the appearance of a mischievous schoolboy. He hooked the bag deftly with the three remaining fingers of his left hand had eased it gently into her cart beside the other groceries.

Before she could answer or thank him, he added, "just give me a minute to grab my groceries and I'll load these into the car for you." She hesitated as she appraised her benefactor, returned his smile and answered, "that's alright, I think I can manage."

Ellen noted that not only was he missing a limb and two fingers on one hand, but both of his arms evidenced scars from previous injuries. In spite of the disfigurement, his appearance held a boyish charm that she found hard to resist. He paid for his meager groceries and put the two additional plastic bags and his crutch into her cart with a smile.

"You lead, I'll follow," he instructed as he commandeered her cart. "I'll use the cart to lean on, I hate the crutch."

She walked slowly, partly to accommodate her diminished

lung capacity and partly for her new friend who hopped along behind her. She towed her oxygen bottle behind her, tethered to the long plastic tube which provided air to the necklace around her neck and into her nose. One who watched would have either been amused or felt pity for the odd couple as they crossed the blacktop before pausing beside a small green Subaru Outback with handicapped plates.

"I'm Ellen," she offered as the tall, young man unloaded her groceries into her car from the shopping cart.

"I'm Lance," he answered smiling broadly, "but my friends at the VA call me **Hopper**."

She laughed musically then said, "thank you for your help **Hopper**."

"My pleasure ma'am," he replied sincerely. "I'll follow you home and unload them."

Involuntarily fear gripped her as she realized she really knew nothing about this man or his motives.

"That's a good pickup line but I'm sure I can handle it myself," she answered. "Besides, I've got some errands to run before I go home."

He seemed disappointed by her tone and answered, "Okay, but you better be quick about them... your ice cream, milk, and butter will not stand much time in a hot car."

She hesitated.

Seconds later she looked over at a huge red pickup truck parked beside her car and noted the Purple Heart emblem on the license plates and the Semper Fi decal across the rear window.

"That's gotta be yours," she said pointing at it. "Big man – big truck."

The remark didn't carry the light-hearted message she

intended but instead broke the bond they'd enjoyed and caused him to frown.

"Maybe we'll meet again," he said over his shoulder as he turned and hopped toward the big Ford.

"I'm sorry, it's just that you are a foot taller than me and your ride seemed a good fit for you," she explained quickly. "I really appreciate your offer to help with the groceries."

He turned back toward her and smiled his infectious smile and said, "well, then lead on and we'll get the job done before your ice cream melts."

He followed closely behind her in the raised truck and parked at the curb as she turned into the driveway and stopped. He stayed in the truck for a few moments before walking carefully across her lawn, now sporting his prostatic limb.

"Can't get used to the thing," he explained, "but it makes some things a lot easier and people around me more comfortable."

He filled his long arms with plastic bags and followed her inside, where he sat them on the kitchen counter. "I'll grab the rest while you put them away," he suggested as he left the room and headed back to her car.

She finished putting the groceries away as he stood awkwardly against the counter, trying to decide how to say goodbye.

"Well **Hopper**, how about a bowl of ice cream for your hard work?" she smiled as she took two bowls from the cupboard and the new half gallon of Ben and Jerry's back from the freezer.

Lance hesitated, smiled and took a seat on a bar stool at the counter. "Yes ma'am, that'd be just fine. A fella once gave me some good advice – he said – *to reject the gift is to reject the giver*."

"That's scriptural I think," Ellen said as she scooped ice cream into the waiting bowls. "I think it refers to Jesus' gift of eternal life given to us through His sacrifice... cookies?" She placed a saucer of cookies on the counter and took the vacant stool beside him.

They ate silently, both no doubt trying to think of the right words to say. Finally, Ellen broke the ice.

"I have a hole in my heart," she admitted. "My mother died of the same thing in her thirties. It's working at something just under 50% capacity the doctors say,. I was born that way they think, but it's getting worse quickly now."

"What can they do about it?" he asked. "Can it be fixed?"

She hesitated before answering. "They say probably so but the cost is outrageous and I lost my insurance when I had to quit my job and with that, lost access to medical coverage. I'll have to get another job and wait until I qualify for benefits now before I can go in."

Alarm was apparent in his voice when he said, "you could die before that and besides, who would hire you knowing you needed surgery and would be off work for an extended time of healing after just being hired?"

Ellen just shrugged.

"Marry me," he blurted without hesitation. "You'll have immediate dependant benefits and we can have it done right away."

She just stared at him for a moment and said, "I don't even know your last name or you mine; why would you do that for me?"

"In war you don't think about how you benefit from doing what is right, you just do what is necessary because it is right," he answered.

"Is that how you lost your leg, doing what needed to be done?" she asked quietly.

"No... yes, well indirectly maybe. I was serving my country, trying to protect the weak from the strong... our Humvee hit an

IED, game over," he answered, while shaking his head.

They continued to talk into the evening, sent out for a pizza, and watched a movie while sitting on opposite ends of her old sofa. It was comfortable, not a boy-girl thing, but more of a friend thing. Both were reaching out, needing something from the other without really knowing what it was.

"How come you are not married?" Lance finally asked. "A bright, pretty girl like you... I'd have thought some guy would already have a ring on your finger."

"I've been asked," she answered, "more than once, but it was never quite right, the timing or the person or something that kept me from saying yes. How about you?"

He seemed to be thinking how to answer before he said, "my Mom and Dad died in a house fire when I was still in high school. I have no brothers or sisters and my aunt and uncle took me in until I graduated. I joined the army right after graduation and stayed there until the IED sent me home. I guess I never really had time to have a proper girlfriend or to fall in love."

Over the next several months they dated, well, not really dated but spent many hours and days together, usually just visiting and talking. One day she asked, "would you really?"

"Would I really what?" he asked, puzzled.

"Marry me," she answered quickly. "Would you really marry me just so I can get the medical help I need?"

"In a minute. Why... have you been considering my proposal?" he asked.

"I have," she admitted quietly. "What about sex?"

Lance was speechless for a moment, then smiled awkwardly and said, "what about it? Do you mean would I expect you to act like a wife in that respect?"

"I've never..." she began letting her voice trail off.

"I haven't either," he answered quickly. "It's almost as if it was by some design, huh?"

At that moment they could have easily been two preteens discussing the forbidden subject as they were rapidly approaching puberty.

A week later he was called to the ER where Ellen had been taken and was told to take a seat and wait for the doctor. As he waited, and fearing the worst, he admitted to himself that he had fallen in love with her and promised God that if she survived he'd marry her.

"Mr. Hogue?" the tall man in green scrubs asked, as he walked toward Lance.

Lance stood. "Yes sir," he said, as though the man was a commanding general.

"Ellen is stable and has asked for you," he said. "Please follow me."

They walked down a long hallway, then turned and walked through double doors labeled ICU, then continued to a curtained-off area to a bed framed by equipment with blinking lights where Ellen lay. Her nose and mouth were covered with a clear plastic mask which was delivering pure oxygen to her, while a pair of nurses hovered nervously nearby. Her eyes were closed, a quick glance at the doctor told Lance everything he needed to know.

"We're getting married today," he said. "Can you arrange for a quiet ceremony here in her room?"

The doctor started to object, then nodded. "It'll have to be brief with no more than two people in the room – we need room to do our jobs."

"One hour," Lance said over his shoulder as he left. "I'll be back in one hour with the Chaplain."

On the drive in, Lance was on the phone to the VA office asking for the Chaplain. When he arrived, he was ushered into his office where he pleaded his case.

"It must be today," he said. "She'll not last another week without the operation."

"But..." the Chaplain began.

"But nothing, sir," Lance said a little too loudly. "I went when my country called and now I'm calling for help from my country. Will you do it or not?"

The officer didn't take offense at the soldier's tone but instead nodded and smiled wanly. "What can I do?" he asked, "what do you need?"

"Cut through the red tape so we can get it done and get her transferred to the VA hospital for immediate surgery. Pull whatever strings you have to help us out," he answered.

"I'll call over to the hospital and see who is available on an emergency basis and how soon they can get her in," he said, picking up his phone. "I'll meet you at the hospital."

Lance left, then went by his apartment, changed into his dress uniform, and drove to the hospital. As he arrived, the Chaplain was just getting out of his car. They walked in together.

When they entered, Ellen opened her eyes, looked curiously at Lance, and tried to smile without much success. Tears were in his eyes when he held up his mother's ring for her to see before asking, "will you marry me?"

She nodded while the Chaplain visited with the staff, asking if they would serve as witnesses. He received positive replies. He moved toward the bedside and looked down at a paper with their names on it and began to speak.

"Will you, Ellen Gray, take Lance Hogue to be your husband? If you will, please nod your head," he said.

She nodded.

"Will you, Lance Hogue, take Ellen Gray to be your wife?" he asked, looking at **Hopper**.

"I will," he answered.

"Then, by the power given me by God and man, I declare you to be husband and wife. May this union be eternally filled with joy," he said. "You may kiss your bride when the time is more appropriate."

The emergency operation wasn't completed until well after midnight and even then, the surgeons were very skeptical of her chances of survival. She stayed in intensive care for 16 days before finally being transferred to a hospital room where she slowly began to improve. Lance was by her side nearly day and night, hardly leaving even to eat or change clothes.

"So, we are really married," she said a week later. "I had always looked forward to a different kind of honeymoon."

"I've never seen this smart-aleck side of you," he responded, laughing. "Maybe I don't know you as well as I thought."

"But you will," she promised. "You are stuck with me now for better or worse."

Each day they bantered back and forth for hours while she continued to improve. Then finally the day came when she could be discharged. He wheeled her out of the door to a new vehicle waiting for them at the curb. He answered her unasked question. "I sold the truck and bought something lower and more comfortable," he said, referring to the new SUV into which he was now helping her get comfortable.

Just the ride home exhausted Ellen. When they pulled the

new vehicle into her driveway, she was already asleep. Lance carefully picked her up and carried her into the house and laid her down in her bed. She opened her eyes, smiled and said, "you carried me across the threshold," before going back to sleep.

Two weeks later she was able to walk, although carefully, and sit across the table from him while he served them breakfast.

"We need to decide if we should move into my apartment or stay here, what you think?" he asked.

"I've lived here my entire life," she answered. "This was my mother's house."

"So you own it?" he said. "That explains a lot. You probably wouldn't want to leave."

"Not unless we were **really** married and we bought our own home," she said laughing.

Her comment brought a frown to **Hopper's** face. "We are **really married** as far as I am concerned... can't you see that I love you?" he said.

"Sorry," she said apologetically. "It kind of felt like it was a **mercy marriage** where you were just doing your duty. It all happened so fast that I still can hardly believe it happened."

"So, you're saying you don't have feelings for me?" he asked.

"No, no, I mean yes..." she pleaded, with tears filling her eyes. "I love everything about you!"

He took her in his arms and for the first time they kissed, gently but passionately.

When they finally finished kissing, he said breathlessly, "this just might work out."

~   ~

Three years later, **Hopper** had remodeled and added on to the old house, and Ellen had recovered from her surgery and has gone back to work full time.

"I think we are pregnant," she said quietly one evening as they sat down for dinner together.

Lance hesitated for a moment while trying to grasp what he had just heard, then smiled sheepishly and answered, "what'll we name her?"

"What makes you think it's a her?" she asked.

"I've been praying for a little girl just like her mommy," he said.

"You've been praying?" she asked in a surprised voice. "I didn't know that."

"There's probably still a lot we don't know about each other, but given time we'll get around to it – in another forty or fifty years," he grinned.

"So, you wanted a baby. A baby girl?" Ellen asked.

"Yup, and a couple of boys too, if that suits you," he answered.

She stood, walked around the table, sat down in his lap and kissed him and said, "*Hopper*, you're a keeper."

Later, an ultra-sound confirmed his prediction. Ellen was nearly twenty weeks pregnant and their baby appeared to be a little girl. The spare bedroom which they had added was now quickly turned into a nursery, with pink and white polka-dotted curtains. They began to collect various baby items as opportunity and finances provided. *Hopper* also got a full-time job working in Veteran's Services, in anticipation of the need for additional in-come. Life, it seemed, was just as God had decreed.

Seven months and three days after Ellen had announced her pregnancy to him, she delivered a beautiful red-haired baby girl, weighing just less than seven pounds. The delivery had gone well and their doctor had pronounced little Amy Jo healthy and eager to enjoy life. Without either pair of grandparents to advise them, they sought advice from several young couples in their church who were already raising families. Tips, both good and bad, gave them direction, and together they developed what they hoped were good workable habits that allowed them to raise Amy Jo in a way which pleased God.

~   ~

At age two, AJ, as they called her, was a handful. Precocious and full of questions, walking or running everywhere, and causing them to question if they were really up to raising more children. The question, however, answered itself a few months later when another ultra-sound supplied evidence of a second pregnancy. Dr. Barnes, who had entered the room smiling, turned his attention to **Hop** and asked, "didn't I overhear you a couple of years ago saying you wanted a couple of sons?"

Lance returned his smile and answered, "that is what I said alright, do we have one?"

The old doctor frowned, hesitated, then said, "I'm afraid not," before then continuing, with the smile returning to his face. "You have two."

"Two?" Ellen questioned. "Are you sure? We have no twins in my family, I thought twins were hereditary."

"My mom was a twin," **Hopper** interjected. "Her sister died as a child, I never knew her."

"It often skips a generation," Dr. Barnes confirmed, shaking his head while still smiling. "Congratulations."

The boys were born right on schedule, God's schedule, at what the doctor had determined was nine months. James and John entered the world after thirteen hours of labor, which no doubt would have killed Ellen if not for the heart surgery five years earlier. They were named after two of the apostles in the

Bible and were the joy of AJ's life.

She mothered them and spent a great deal of her time sitting beside them talking quietly, no doubt schooling them on what they should expect when they were as old as she. Ironically, they would always stop crying and seemed to listen to what she had to say. Both **Hop** and Ellen longed for the grandparents and family they both lacked with which to share their joy.

AJ was four and her brothers a year old when Ellen returned to working weekends on a part-time basis, leaving her precious family in the care of her husband. They had agreed that as soon as the construction cost of the third bedroom was paid, she could return home to care full-time for their growing family.

Snowfall came early that year, much to AJ's delight, arriving just before Halloween. She could be heard in a hushed voice in her brother's bedroom, explaining how white flakes of snow mysteriously fell silently from heaven for children to play with. Although uncomprehending, they would always listen quietly, as their red-haired mentor explained to them the secrets of the universe.

Lance was not overly concerned but curious when he observed the first set of boot prints in the fresh snow coming up their sidewalk and stopping at the front door, before leaving back down the walkway, without any attempt to contact those inside. In his former military life, such an unannounced visit would have been called a recon. But, he reasoned, a recon for what purpose?

"Have you seen anyone prowling around our yard?" Lance asked Ellen one evening.

A look of concern filled her face before she answered. "No, why do you ask?"

"Probably nothing," he smiled wanly. "Twice since the snow fall, we have had a visit from someone who came to the front door but decided not to ring the doorbell."

"Maybe just kids," she offered.

"No," he answered firmly. "It was an adult's shoe print."

They didn't discuss it further, but both felt unsettled by his discovery.

~ ~

With AJ in the first grade and the twins walking and talking incessantly, the Hogue family now seemed to have little quiet time together. It appeared that life had caught up with the young, carefree couple, who had had such a short time alone together before beginning their lives in such a remarkable way.

Ellen was at the market shopping when she first noticed him. AJ was pushing the shopping cart with an air of importance while she followed behind with her sons in a double stroller. Not that they couldn't have walked, but more so she could maintain control of them while she shopped. She first noticed him in the produce department, giving her a sidewise glance, as he inspected the vegetables. She could have attributed his interest to her youthful beauty and the return of her trim figure but she did not. She felt uncomfortable and ill at ease.

She was buckling the children into their car seats in the parking lot when he stopped beside her, smiled, and offered to help her load her groceries. She returned his smile but quickly declined his offer before driving away.

"There was this man..." Ellen began, visibly shaken, "at the super market, he was creepy."

"I'll be right home!" *Hopper* answered quickly, before jumping to his feet at work and leaving the building.

When he arrived at home, Ellen was still visibly shaken, although she could not say for certain just why. The children had also picked up on the fact that something was not quite right, but of course had no idea what it was.

"Did he say or do anything to directly frighten you?" **Hop** asked.

"No, certainly nothing I can prove, it is more like a feeling I had when I caught him looking at us. A feeling that his interest in us was not well intentioned," she tried to explain. She could see concern in her husband's eyes and for the first time in their years together, anger.

"Describe him," **Hop** asked, in a tone that was close to an order. "Have you ever seen him before?

She hesitated, thinking for several moments before answering in a shaky voice, "he kind of looks like the UPS driver."

Hop, of course, had not had any reason to pay attention to the man who delivered an occasional package, and for the most part, had left it on the step beside the door with no interaction with the family.

Lance felt himself relax a bit and said in a less serious voice "maybe he recognized you from his route and was just trying to be friendly."

Ellen considered what he had said before trying to smile and put the incident out of her mind. Sure, she thought, he was staring at us trying to remember where he'd seen us before, she reasoned.

Hopper himself, however, couldn't get rid of the nagging feeling that those tracks in the snow were somehow tied to the event at the store. A week later, he was coming home from work at the Veterans Hospital when he saw the UPS van parked a few blocks from his house. He pulled in behind it and got out. The sun had already gone down and the final vestiges of light were quickly fading as he approached the side door of the vehicle. The door was open, the driver sitting in his seat filling out papers for his final delivery.

"Hi," ***Hop*** said as he entered the van. "I live a few blocks over and wanted to have a word with you."

"I know who you are, get out of my van!" was the driver's harsh reply. ***Hop*** turned and attempted to step back out onto the sidewalk as he'd been told, but was hit from behind with a heavy object.

"Get up, war hero! Let's see how well you can fight. You make me sick parading around in uniform, drawing a disability check for being in the wrong place at the wrong time, while they gave me a dishonorable and threw me out for killing too many rag heads. I'm going to kill you and become the daddy to that little family of yours," the big man said, while looking contemptuously down at ***Hopper***.

For a few seconds ***Hopper*** lay on his face on the rough cement while fury, long repressed, filled every part of him. He got to his feet and took note that the man was every bit as large as he, and more heavily muscled. As the battle began, it was apparent that both men had been well trained in the art of hand to hand combat. What the driver had said was quite possibly the wrong thing to say, and almost certainly the wrong person to whom to say it.

A feigned punch, followed by a crashing blow, staggered ***Hopper*** before a glancing kick to his head dropped him to his knees. This is as real as it gets, his mind told him. Kill or be killed. With his life and the lives of his family in the balance, ***Hop*** disconnected a small telescoping baton, much like the police use, which had been attached to the outside of his artificial leg.

For the first time ***Hopper*** spoke mockingly to his opponent, "maybe we should even the playing field a little" as he struck the big man in his left knee, nearly causing him to fall, while bellowing in pain.

Warily, they circled each other for several minutes while exchanging blows, before the driver charged him like a mad bull with his head down. As he lifted **Hop** from his feet, **Hop** heaved upward with both hands under the man's muscled neck until he heard it break and the body collapsed beneath him. His lifeless body fell to the pavement, just as the black and white cruiser pulled up with lights flashing.

The homeowner who had called them was standing in his doorway motioning to the two combatants. "I saw it all, the driver attacked the guy in uniform," he yelled.

It took over an hour for the police to take everyone's statements after the ambulance had removed the body. By that time Ellen had left the children with a neighbor and driven to the scene, following her husband's call.

"Life is uncertain" **Hopper** said, as they lay in their darkened bedroom hours later. "Not all who die in war fall on the battlefield."

Pathways, Trails, and Stepping Stones

Life is a gift given by God to be enjoyed and appreciated without knowing either its duration or what events may define it. Our choices do not alter its ultimate outcome but certainly contribute to the joy we encounter while living it.

~ ~

Dimples: those mysterious and alluring little dents in the cheeks or chin which add character and charm to their hosts' faces.

Miriam was, from the beginning, precocious and energetic, with an insatiable curiosity and a fearless spirit. Her overly large blue eyes were set in a soft baby face that seemed, and no doubt was, conceived in Heaven. Her round little face was accented with dimples on both cheeks and at the point, if there had been a point, of her chubby little chin.

Blake and Miriam had been high school sweethearts, who had grown up together and had it not been for the call of duty which led him to join the army, would have probably married right out of high school. Instead however, they parted ways, with her going off to college and him to Iraq. They stayed in touch periodically with an occasional letter, and met the few times that he returned home on leave between tours, but saw each other less and less as the years passed. She dated, although not seriously, while he concentrated on keeping himself and his comrades-in-arms alive on the opposite side of the world.

When the news came, it was already too late for Blake to secure emergency leave and make it home before his father passed. He was, however, able to make it in time for the funeral. His 30-day leave had begun the day he had boarded the plane home, which took a full day to get him stateside, and the best part of a second on a commercial airline, before he finally walked into his childhood home.

His mother, sister, and his two uncles and their wives and families were gathered inside, laughing and talking, as though the event was some kind of family reunion, to which he took immediate offense. "He's dead, for hell's sake," he thought. "What could be so damn amusing?" Tom was only 46 when he'd been stricken by a massive heart attack and had not survived the night. Blake rebuffed their efforts to greet him, using the excuse that he needed to get some sleep, and went to his old room. When Blake finally lay down on the bed, he'd expected to have to have had trouble sleeping, but found that both his body and his mind were indeed exhausted and soon was fast asleep. The long trip and the emotion of the event had taken its toll on him.

Familiar faces all, but seemingly from another world and time, were gathered around the graveside. Some with red eyes, others with somber, expressionless faces, as the pastor read the short account of Tom's life. Blake mused at how any man's life could be summed up in so few words, as he listened dispassionately as the old reverend read the obituary. Beside him, his mother and sister stood woodenly, shivering in the cold fall wind, sobbing involuntarily. He raised his head and found himself looking into Miriam's moist blue eyes as she stood with her family across from him, on the other side of the open grave. He'd nearly forgotten how beautiful she was until she tried bravely to smile at him, with tears now running down her cheeks.

Pain filled his heart, repressed pain from a thousand moments in time where he'd had neither the time nor luxury to allow it. Tears filled his own eyes as he realized he'd never again have opportunity to speak with his father, to ask *man* questions or share his own life experiences with him. He began to sob, softly at first, then more and more until his entire body was racked with emotion. He emptied himself into his hands before walking slowly away from the cluster of grieving people standing at the graveside. Seemingly far away, the drone of the old preacher's voice continued its steady monotone.

Miriam touched his arm gently without speaking, knowing her presence alone would be of some comfort to him. Blake composed himself before acknowledging her beside him.

"Thank you," he said, knowing she'd understand the full meaning which the brief statement held.

She slid her hand into the crook of his elbow and smiled sadly up at him, without answering. He noted she still had her childhood dimples and deep blue eyes, but had now become a beautiful young woman. How, he wondered, and why, had they never pursued the love he knew they had felt for each other. They walked without speaking, just enjoying the comfort they each felt being together once again.

"How long will you be home," she finally asked, as they seated themselves on a bench under a tree, among endless rows of granite markers.

"I have thirty days," he answered, shaking his head, while secretly wondering how anyone could get over the death of their father in a month's time. "You?"

"I have most of the summer off. I teach school now and we go back to work the last week in August," she answered.

He marveled privately that she'd made a life for herself outside of their relationship. He had supposed that she would stay frozen in time awaiting his return so they could marry and live happily ever after. It occurred to him now that she was wearing an engagement ring on her left hand, with a huge solitaire diamond. He nodded toward it and asked, "someone special?"

She smiled sadly at him and answered quietly, "I hope so."

"Do I know him?" he persisted.

"I doubt it, he's from back east, we met in grad school a year or so ago," she answered honestly.

About the time her letters slowed, then finally stopped coming, Blake thought to himself. He knew he'd been lax in keeping in communication with her and had made a thousand excuses to himself, which justified his lack of commitment.

"How's your family?" Blake asked, changing the subject. "Are they well?"

Miriam smiled, then said, "Eva got married and is pregnant. I'm going to be an aunt." Then her face changed when she added, "Mom has breast cancer and they say it's just a matter of time. Dad and Tommy are having trouble dealing with it."

"I'm so sorry," he said, his eyes brimming with tears. "I didn't know."

"Of course you didn't, how could you? I didn't want to bother you knowing there was nothing you could do but worry," she said.

"I do think she'd love to see you though, if you have time."

"I have time," he said with resignation. "She was always just like a mother to me."

Miriam smiled sadly, then nodded, but said nothing.

A few hundred feet away, Blake could see people leaving the graveside and walking toward their cars. His mother and sister stood together, searching the crowd, he supposed for him.

"I've gotta go," he said, as he stood and began to walk toward where his father's body would spend eternity. "Mom's waiting for me."

She watched as he crossed the grassy lawn and caught the eyes of his mother and sister, and put his arms around them. She too wondered why they hadn't begun a life together.

"Morning sleepy head," his mother said, as he walked into the kitchen where she was busily preparing breakfast.

The familiar sounds and smells of home brought back fond memories of a childhood filled with the security of believing that it would always be so, before the crushing knowledge that his Dad would not walk into the room and give his mother a peck on the cheek and say "good morning beautiful."

"Smells good," Blake said, trying to sound enthusiastic. "What's for breakfast?"

"Waffles, bacon and eggs," she answered smiling, before adding, "your Dad's fav...." Her voice trailed off at the thought that he wouldn't be joining them.

Blake tried hard to overlook what he knew she'd tried to say, but the dagger in his heart filled him with pain. Neither of them spoke for several minutes, while she tried to look busy turning the bacon and then frying the eggs in the bacon grease.

The elephant in the room grew larger and larger and the silence deafening, until it seemed to suffocate them.

Jana, Blake's sister, joined them as naturally as light follows darkness, gave him a kiss on top of his head and sat down beside him. "'Sup Bro?" she asked, trying to sound like some illiterate from the hood.

She had grown what seemed to him like a foot since he'd been home last, although she still was just barely five feet tall and approaching eighteen years old.

"How's school going?" he asked, for a lack of something to say.

"School's out for the summer, dummy," she laughed, "but I'm on track to graduate next year, with no problems."

"What are you going to be *if* you ever grow up?" he asked, purposely chiding her.

"I'm thinking if I get a basketball scholarship, I'll go to college and get drafted into the WBA," she answered smiling. "Or maybe a nurse." How like his little sister, he thought, light hearted and carefree, not a clue – no plan, taking life as it came. He envied her ability to live life without worrying.

He was tall and spare, built like his father, and had been a starter all three years in high school as a point guard. He'd likely have been offered a scholarship to play ball if he'd not have joined the service. She, on the other hand, was built just like their mother Jean, short and diminutive, but with a lust for life and a larger than life spirit.

"Working?" he asked her as their Mom put the food on the table and joined them.

"I'm a dog walker," she announced proudly.

"A what?" he answered.

Jana rolled her eyes to show him he was 'out of the loop', then explained, "all of the new people moving to town seem to have more money than brains. They buy these fancy dogs, then pay someone to exercise them. I get $20 an hour and sometimes walk two or three at a time. Not bad for a high school kid, huh?"

Blake smiled and whistled. "And I mowed lawns for five bucks plus tips," he said, putting on a pouty face.

He caught his mother smiling out of the corner of his eye, no doubt reliving the memory of him as a kid. For just a moment, the room was once again filled with happiness, before his mother spoke again.

"Did Miriam tell you about her mother?" she asked quietly.

"Yeah, said it was bad," he answered. "I plan to run over there later today and see her."

They busied themselves with breakfast, not speaking for several minutes, before Jana asked, "are you going to get the Mustang running while you are home?"

Blake hadn't thought of his pride and joy in a long time. He'd driven a 1969 Mustang Mach I in high school and put it in the garage under a tarp when he left for Iraq.

"Maybe," he answered, smiling. "But I may need a little help getting it cleaned up, and I don't pay twenty bucks an hour," he laughed.

"I just happen to have a few hours available in my busy schedule," she said, sticking out her tongue at him, much like she'd have done when she was eight years old.

When they stood and began taking their dishes to the sink their Mom spoke. "You kids go on along now, I'll take care of that. It gives me something to do."

By her tone, Blake could tell that she was looking ahead to many long days alone, with little to do and no husband to share them with.

Blake was 18 again as they pulled back the tarp, revealing the pristine old Ford. The excitement of ownership and the pride that went with it gave him a feeling that he, like the car, was unique in its own way – that feeling had made them nearly inseparable. He had washed it almost daily and waxed it weekly, never letting it look less than its best.

He knew it's stats by heart, 310 HP, 4:10 rear end with a close ratio four speed, shaker air scoop, bucket seats, and pin stripes. It all came back in an instant, the point gap, the spark plugs, timing 8 degrees advanced... the whole enchilada. For a moment, he wondered what the attraction to Desert Storm had really been. Had he been running away from something, or just stretching his wings as young men sometimes do?

He'd of course taken out the battery, which would have long since gone bad anyway, and put new fresh oil in the crankcase. A check of the dip stick showed it to still look like honey.

"We'll need a battery," he said, more or less to himself.

"And some fresh gas," Jana added. "Did you drain the tank before you parked it?

Blake was surprised ay how much his sister seemed to have picked up from him or their Dad over the years. "Yeah, I drained the tank and emptied the carb so it wouldn't varnish up," he answered. "I hope the gaskets haven't dried out too much.

"Who's running the shop?" Blake asked his sister as they drove their Dad's truck to the parts store. He was, of course, referring to the family business.

"Bill is still there, he's the manager now, and Tommy and Ben both work part-time, running parts and picking up the slack. Dad did most of the tune-ups and PR to keep the people happy, and Mom does the books."

Bill was Miriam's father and Tommy his son, Blake did not

remember Ben but assumed he was also a young man like Tommy, trying to learn the trade.

They stopped and parked, then went inside. A new face at the counter greeted Blake before a yell from the back room got his attention. Sean ran toward them with a million-dollar smile pasted across his freckled face.

He bear-hugged Blake, lifting him off his feet, then set him down and said, "great to see you old friend, didn't have a chance to talk to you at the funeral. We were so sorry to hear about Tom."

Sean was of Irish heritage and as such sported curly red hair and had pasty white skin, with a multitude of freckles. He'd been Blake's friend since grade school and the center on their high school basketball team. Of course, he'd filled out and other than his six-foot six height, didn't much resemble the tall lanky kid Blake had always known.

Sean answered the unasked question, "we own the store, or will someday after we pay off old Gene. I have two guys working for me," he continued proudly.

Blake nodded, "who's we?" he asked.

"Guess you didn't know, Mary Ellen and I got married two years ago," he explained. "She's pregnant now with our second. Are you gonna get the old 'stang runnin'?" he asked.

"That's why we're here," Blake answered. "I need a battery, maybe a carb kit, and a place to buy some good gas."

"95 octane is about as good as it gets these days, but I can give you a can of booster to add to the tank," Sean said. "Chevron is the only place in town that does not add ethanol to their gas."

He set the new battery on the counter, then asked, "do you want to take the kit with you or just have me make sure I have one in stock?" Of course, he was already checking inventory on the computer as he spoke.

"Got 'er, just let me know if you need 'er," Sean offered, speaking of the kit.

Blake paid for the battery and had just turned to leave when Sean spoke again. "We're living in Mom and Dad's old house, bought it from them when they moved to the city, we'd love to have you come by and see us."

"I'll make it a point to," Blake smiled. "I want to see Mary Ellen and your little one."

He and Jana left and drove to the Chevron and filled the GI can with premium before stopping at the A&W to get an ice cream cone on their way home.

"I could get used to having you around," Jana said with a smile.

He returned her smile but instantly felt a pang of sadness when he remembered why he was home.

'The shop' as it had been referred, was the auto mechanic shop that Tom had always run. It had been a fixture in the small town and a place the locals could always depend on to fix their vehicles. Blake worked there growing up, first mopping and cleaning the restrooms, sweeping the office and emptying trash, then running the lube bay and putting up tools. Later, when his Dad taught him the mechanical side, he found it a perfect fit and most probably why he had ended up in the motor pool in the military.

Blake poured all but a cup or so of the fuel into the tank, took off the coil wire and cranked the big motor over. His theory was to lubricate the cylinder walls and pump fuel to the carburetor before trying to start it. When he replaced the wire, the old motor started right up without priming, but ran roughly for several minutes at an idle, before settling down to a nice even 700 RPM's. A hint of gas was visible along the gaskets in the carb before they drank in enough gasoline to swell and seal themselves. Blake checked and aired the tires, then turned the car off and rechecked the oil level on the dipstick.

"Ready for a ride?" he asked his sister.

Her smile answered his question as she climbed into the waiting car. It felt good to be behind the wheel again, he thought, looking at the familiar dash and instruments clustered before him. For a moment he was eighteen again and Miriam, not Jana, was sitting beside him as they backed down the driveway from the garage. The Mustang was a far cry from the Humvee which he drove everyday a half a world away. It was light on its feet and ready to run, hitting 60 easily before he shifted to third.

"Careful big Bro," Jana warned. "You don't want to attract too much attention, your license plates are three years old."

He smiled and eased off the pedal until he was under the speed limit. "Good idea," he said. "I'd hate to get to know the local Sheriff all over again."

When they returned home, their mother was sitting on the front porch with an empty chair beside her. And so it would always be, Blake realized. The Mustang sat at the curb, its waxed finish glistening in the afternoon sun, which belied that it hadn't been washed in years.

"Looks good," Jean commented, as she nodded her head toward the car. "Did you drive by the shop and show her off?"

"Naw, killjoy here reminded me my plates were expired," Blake answered, nudging his kid sister. "I don't want to ruin the family reputation."

"You did that when you were 16," she countered. "You were the terror of Tremonton."

It was after 5:00 when he pulled the Mustang into Miriam's

driveway, with apprehension filling his heart. He'd once cared for Grace a great deal, she'd been almost a second Mom, the very thought of her dying seemed like salt in the recent wound that his Dad's death had caused. Bill answered the door looking tired but pleased to see him.

"Come on in Blake," he said as he stood aside, "you are always welcome here."

Blake remembered a time, which now seemed so long ago, when he'd not have stopped to knock, but would have walked right in. Grace was sitting on the sofa wearing an oxygen necklace, with a walker parked beside her. Tommy walked somberly up and gave Blake a man hug and handshake. The gloom of the reality of imminent death filled the small living room, just as it had filled Blake's mind on the long flight back home. Miriam stood silently in the background, her eyes brimming with tears. Grace made a feeble effort to stand before settling back on the sofa with resignation.

"It's so good to see you Blake," she said smiling wanly, "it's been too long."

Blake walked to her, leaned down and took her frail body in his arms, and gave her a gentle hug before answering. "Yes it has Grace, I only wish I'd never have left."

He surprised himself at the unplanned words he'd just uttered, while wondering where they had come from. As he raised his eyes, they looked into Miriam's.

Two couples from the church brought dinner, but stayed only a short time to offer prayers of encouragement before leaving. He sat beside Miriam and took her hand as Bill blessed the meal, feeling the ring on her hand as he did. To his surprise, everyone but Grace seemed famished and ate hungrily, without conversation. How many times, he thought, had he sat in this very chair and looked forward at a life certain, that it would include these three people.

After Grace retired to her bedroom, they sat for a long time and visited in muted tones about inconsequential things that held little value to anyone. It was after 10:00 when he walked into his childhood home to find his mother sitting in the living room, reading her Bible.

"How are they doing, honey?" she asked sincerely. "How's Grace?"

"Okay, I guess," Blake said, while wondering what a proper answer would be. "Can I ask you a question, Mom?" nearly choking on his words.

"If you could have chosen, would you have asked for more time with Dad, to have more days and hours to prepare for his death, or would you have asked for it to be over suddenly, just as it happened?" he asked, with tears running down his cheeks.

She looked at him strangely, seemingly trying to absorb and evaluate his question before answering. "I honestly do not know, we had a few hours but those were spent trying to countermand God's perfect will, and delay the inevitable. Only God knows the day and the hour when the time is right to call us home. If it were up to us, we'd never be ready to say goodbye and go to fulfill our purpose in heaven."

When Blake finally closed his eyes and sleep had overtaken him, he was still marveling at the wisdom of his mother's words.

Three days later, Blake met Richard for the first time and had an almost immediate dislike for him. He tried to rationalize if it was because he still loved Miriam and had lost her to him, or if it was because he looked and acted like a self-centered, holier-than-thou, know-it-all. Probably a little of both he finally decided.

The fact that he was from a wealthy family back east, and was several years her senior, of course had little to do with it. Richard was handsome in an effeminate way; tall and tanned, long groomed fingernails, and wore custom-made clothes. A "dandy", he would have been called in earlier days, a shyster and a con man, who had never worked an honest job or had the need to. He could not imagine what Miriam had seen in the man.

Evidently others, including Bill, were also unimpressed because word quickly got around the small town about the stranger who was engaged to Miriam. Unknown to anyone, Bill hired a private investigator to check into the background of his possible future son-in-law and found evidence tying his family to organized crime.

"Blake, would you come down to the shop, I need to visit with you," Bill said into the phone.

"Of course," Blake answered, "anytime that is good for you."

"The sooner the better, and don't mention it to **anyone**," Bill cautioned.

On the drive down, Blake wondered if possibly Grace had gotten worse and Bill needed his support.

"Please sit down," Bill said, while motioning to a chair by his desk, as he closed the office door.

"I'll come right to the point," Bill said, his face reddening. "What is your opinion of Richard?"

"Well I..." Blake started, trying to be honest but still not come across as the jilted lover.

"Don't you "**well I**" me... I've known you since you were a baby, tell me what you think," Bill urged.

Blake took a deep breath and let it all go, telling the full truth about what he thought of the man with whom he had shared so little time.

"Well said," Bill said smiling, "those are my thoughts exactly, and... do you still have feelings for Miriam?"

Again, Blake hesitated.

"Do you still love her or not?" Bill persisted. "Are you willing to fight for her?"

It seemed like hours as Blake dug deep into his heart for an answer while Bill waited. Finally, he answered, "like whip him or kill him?"

For the first time Bill laughed before saying, "neither, it will be harder than that. You'll have to show her who he really is without coming across as the guy who wants her back. It will have to be her decision to dump him."

"You hurt her badly you know," Bill continued. "She'd have waited all of her life for you if she knew how deeply you cared about her. But it is not too late, just *be* who you are. She's smart enough to see through him, given half a chance."

"Do you know more than you are telling me?" Blake asked, suddenly picking up on the urgency Bill was projecting.

Again, Bill smiled, "you read me pretty well. You very well may be in danger if you challenge him outright... his family is connected."

"Connected... as in mob?" Blake asked.

"That's what I gather," Bill answered. "I had him checked out."

Richard had, of course, reserved the best suite in town and disdained to spend but a minimum of time with Miriam and her family at their home. When he did, it was almost noticeable how he hated to sit on their furniture, as though he might catch something. He showed no affection to either her nor her family while they were there. Blake saw it as the perfect place for him to reveal what kind of a man he really was.

"Mom, how would you feel about going with me to visit Grace and Bill?" he asked in a cavalier tone.

"I'd love it," she answered enthusiastically. "Did I ever tell you she and I were roommates before your Dad and I met? **Besties** is what Jana calls it now, best friends."

"Let's take them dinner and stay and eat and visit with them" he suggested, as his plan began to come together. "Maybe Miriam and her fiancé will join us."

"Should I make something fancy?" she asked, while trying to formulate a menu.

"No, just good old home cooking like we all used to enjoy. Maybe pot roast, mashed potatoes, and gravy with some of your homemade rolls," he suggested.

"Bill, Mom and I are bringing dinner over tonight if that is alright, we'd like to stay and enjoy it with you and visit awhile, perhaps Richard and Miriam would like to join us," Blake said when he called the shop the next morning.

"I'm sure they would," Bill said chuckling. "I'll call Miriam and ask her."

The old oval table was set for nine which included Tommy and Jana, as well as Bill, Grace, Eva, Blake, Jean, Miriam and Richard. The familiar old mismatched plates were chipped and worn. but the good silver was placed neatly beside them. Eva's husband was not able to make the gathering. Jean had outdone herself roasting a ten-pound sirloin tip, cooked with a dozen potatoes and carrots. Rich brown gravy made from the beef broth and two dozen rolls rounded out the entrée. Two fresh Dutch apple pies with vanilla ice cream more than covered anyone's need for desert.

They were all seated and waiting when Richard and Miriam finally showed up in his Beemer. Richard was introduced around the table before Bill led them in prayer and asked that the Lord bless the food and those in the house. Richard was dressed like a million bucks, sporting a long-sleeved custom-made shirt, expensive shoes, and Armani slacks. Blake, seated next to him, wore a clean T-shirt that advertized Hard Rock Café Bagdad, tennis shoes, and jeans. Looking around the table, others were dressed likewise except Bill, who still wore his shirt from work.

As the food was passed around the table, everyone helped themselves and began eating, laughing and talking all at once. Richard looked stricken, as though he'd joined a group of natives squatted around a campfire. He took only small amounts of each item and pretended to enjoy them as he picked at them with his fork. In the process of buttering his roll, Blake bumped Richard's elbow, causing him to dip his sleeve into the mashed potatoes and gravy on his plate.

"Sorry," Blake said, "my bad." He'd picked up the phrase earlier from Jana and decided it was the perfect time to use it.

Richard took immediate affront, with his face flushed. He stood and headed to the bathroom to wash his shirt sleeve. Blake had to try hard not to laugh when he caught Bill's smile across the table. When he finally returned, Blake noted that both sleeves had been painstakingly rolled up to the elbow.

That Grace and Jean seemed to be having an especially good visit at the far end of the table was duly noted by Miriam, who smiled at Blake and nodded toward them. Enough said, he thought. The evening was a success, whether or not she could see through Richard's fancy exterior. Both women were enjoying themselves.

Miriam and Richard were silent as she drove him back to his

hotel. Finally, he turned toward her and said, "did you see what that clumsy country bumpkin did to my shirt, I think he did it on purpose. This whole trip has been very inconvenient, I cannot imagine how you were ever happy here."

"Great dinner Mom!" Blake and Jana said nearly simultaneously on their drive home. "We should do that again."

She smiled before answering. "I'll talk with Gracie about that.

The ten days since Blake had left the Middle East seemed to have gone by in hyper-drive. With only 20 remaining, he was jealous of each minute and how it was spent. The saving grace of the situation was the quality time that Jean and Grace were spending together, and the vitality that Grace seemed to have compared to when he had first seen her. While still on oxygen, and with a poor long-range prognosis, they had began to take short drives together.

The turning point came when Richard had announced he was returning to Chicago and for Miriam to let him know when it was over and when he should return for the funeral. She was in tears when she told Blake.

"He was as cold as a snake," she said, shaking her head. "I gave him his ring back and told him never to come back. I'll never understand what I ever saw in him."

Blake held her in his arms without speaking, with his heart crying out to tell her that he loved her and wanted to spend his life with her. He did not, instead he remembered Bill's wise counsel to move slowly and let her make her own decisions.

With only a week of his leave left, he contacted his commanding officer and explained his mother's situation, leaving out the romantic attraction he felt for Miriam.

"You have only three months left of your tour, let me make some calls and see if you can finish them up stateside," the Colonel said. "I'll get back to you."

Meanwhile, Grace and Jean had become nearly inseparable, taking short drives and sharing lunches at the local diner or in the park, as Grace's energy allowed. Blake spent his spare time getting his hands greasy, providing help wherever Bill needed it most. As he became reacquainted with the locals and many of the new residents, he fell back into step with the community.

"Sergeant Hogue... Colonel White," the man began. "You have been officially cleared to complete your military commitment stateside. You should receive your orders by the end of the week. Your gear will be shipped to you compliments of the US Army with our thanks for your service."

It was short and sweet but it was all that Blake could have prayed for. He broke the news to his family before calling Miriam and asking her to join him for dinner.

"First and most importantly, I want to apologize for the pain I have caused you," he began, after they were seated and had ordered their meal. "And second, I want to share the news that I will not be returning to Iraq. I have been approved to finish out my enlistment right here. I will get my orders where to report by the end of the week." He hesitated, allowing her to absorb what he had said before continuing.

"I am certain that the love I once felt for you is still there and stronger than ever. What I am uncertain of is what feelings you have for me," he said, pausing for her response.

"Hardly a day," she began carefully, formulating what she wanted to say. "Hardly a day has gone by when I didn't think of you and wonder why we never married. Even after Richard asked me to marry him, I continued to wonder about us."

Excitement filled him as he listened to her, but he sensed a certain reservation in her voice.

"So," she began, cutting right to the chase. "Are you about to ask me to marry you or what?"

Suddenly he was filled with anxiety, he felt like a teenager asking a girl to the prom. Blake began to speak, but then closed his mouth as the words crowded against his lips, like kids waiting for a concert, without organization or order. The fact that she was smiling seemed good, but he could not tell if she was enjoying his misery or waiting for his answer so she could turn him down.

"Yes," he finally answered.

"Yes what?" she persisted, continuing to watch him squirm.

"Yes, I want to ask you to marry me and spend the rest of your life with me," he finally said, with difficulty.

"Yes" she repeated, then hesitated and added, "yes I will."

"When?" he asked. "I was hoping we could do it right away so that both your Mom and Dad could be there." He knew now, more than ever, that time was precious and Grace had little of it.

She picked right up on his urgency, smiled and answered, "Makes sense to me, let's wait until you see what your orders say and we'll go for it. Our honeymoon can wait until you get out of the Army."

He was no longer ill at ease and joked, "you seem to have thought this through already."

"I'm a quick study, who has had years to prepare," she answered, before kissing him gently on the cheek. "Do I get a ring?"

"Oh yeah," he answered, embarrassed by his oversight. "I have it right here."

He fumbled in his pocket and produced a velvet box with a beautiful solitaire inside, about half the size of the one she'd rejected from Richard. He slipped it on her finger and returned her kiss squarely on her lips.

They left with their dinners untouched, paid the bill, and then went home to share the news with her parents. Bill, Grace, and Jean were sitting visiting when they arrived.

"How was dinner?" Bill asked, while giving Blake a wink.

Blake didn't have time to answer, Miriam answered for him. "We are getting married," she said, "just as soon as we have his orders."

Two days later his orders arrived by registered mail. He had two weeks to report to the recruiter's office in Sheridan, which was about fifty miles away. He'd serve out the remainder of his time as a recruiter there. A week later they were married, with family and many friends in attendance, then moved into rented a small apartment. Her sister, Eva, however missed the event because she was delivering a beautiful baby boy.

It is said by the wise that all things happen in God's time and so they do. A short time after Grace was able to hold her grandson in her arms, her health took a turn for the worse. She passed away quietly in her sleep a week later.

Time passed quickly for the newly married couple and before they knew it, school had began and Miriam had accepted a teaching position in the local elementary school. Blake began working at the shop as time permitted, while completing his military commitment. Bill and Jean became co-owners, with Bill continuing to manage the day-to-day operations and Jean keeping the books. Blake eventually began working full time, with Tommy quickly becoming a good mechanic in his own right.

As I bring this story to a close, I am tempted to share the results of the long delayed honeymoon and the subsequent birth of their daughter... but I won't.

A Second Opinion

When the nurse called, I was flippant and unconcerned, totally unaware of how quickly life can change. As she went through the laundry list of individual tests, while reading off values of the results, I paid little attention. They all were within the range that was considered normal, until she hesitated and said, "the doctor wants you to go in for another blood draw so that he can determine the cause of your abnormal bilirubin values."

I hesitated a moment before asking, "my what?"

"Your bilirubin test showed a value which could possibly indicate trouble in your liver," she explained.

I am not rocket scientist, but I still knew that the human liver was an important and necessary organ for good health and a fore-shadowing of worry filled me with fear.

"Is it cancer or something?" I asked the nurse. "Is it a big deal?"

"Just schedule the blood draw and when he gets the results, he will call you," she answered noncommittally. Her unwillingness to answer my question automatically set my mind in motion, and not in a positive way.

I did not mention anything to my wife, I determined that the knowledge would serve little purpose other than to worry her as it had me.

"What did the doctor say?" she asked as soon as I came into

the house. I hedged my bet and answered, trying to sound irritated, "I've got go back in for a blood test, they missed something the first time around, no big deal."

"When?" she asked.

"Whenever I have time, no rush," I answered, still playing the game. "I'll drop by the hospital when I'm in the neighborhood." She seemed to relax and put the matter out of her mind just as I'd hoped, but I on the other hand felt both guilty and anxious to get the results.

"Do you drink?" the doctor asked straightforwardly as soon as he entered the exam room carrying my chart.

Taken off guard, I struggled to answer honestly, "sometimes, when I feel like it."

"How much do you drink?" he asked doggedly. "How much a day?"

"I don't drink every day," I answered proudly. "Mostly only when we have company, or on weekends."

He seemed unsatisfied by my answers and continued, "Okay then, on the average, how many drinks do you consume a week?"

Get off this, I was thinking, I'm not a drunk and I shouldn't have to explain myself to you. But something inside of me was asking the same questions too.

"Maybe a six pack or two on a weekend, one or two a day on the average," I reasoned. "Why do you ask?"

He ignored my question and answered with a question. "Can you quit?"

"Of course I can quit," I answered, proudly taking up the inferred challenge.

He did not blink but smiled and said, "why don't you quit then for a year, then come back and we'll take another look at your liver values?" He turned and left the room, leaving my mouth open ready to argue, but no one with which to argue.

I never did see that doctor again, didn't want to, and didn't need to. I didn't have a single drink of alcohol for the next twelve months, and over the last 30+ years, have drunk only sparingly and infrequently. I learned a lot about myself, my friends, and life over that time, including the fact that drinking **DOES NOT** make you smarter, more attractive, a better dancer, or funnier than you were when you were sober.

It was a shocker to see my friends who, like me, imagined it somehow enhanced their lives. Praise to God I've had no liver problems or other health problems other than those brought on by advancing age.

Searching for Answers

Whether they truly believe in Jesus as their Redeemer or not, most people have an inherent knowledge that God, our Creator, does exist and to varying degrees, are also aware of the Holy Bible. What no one knows is why God began the story at Creation, told it through His prophets and others and then suddenly stopped for several hundred years, only to resume the story with the birth of Christ. My story, while fictional, may cause you to think and consider why you believe that to be so.

It occurs to me that some would view this story as just another "time travel" story; let me explain why I do not believe this is so. God exists outside of time, **how**? We do not know but He does. That said, for Him all things are in His present, and cannot He, as the omnipotent Creator of all things, choose where to place His chess pieces without explaining His motives to anyone?

~   ~

Like many seekers of truth, Clinton was unafraid to invest himself in finding answers to those things for which there appeared to be no answer. As a true believer and Bible scholar, whose job it was to search every word of Scripture and then interpret it for those who would publish new versions of the Word, he did not take his charge lightly. He was young, intelligent, and committed to God, with a ready smile and a giving spirit.

The first time it happened, Clint had packed his laptop, his lunch, and a few miscellaneous papers in a box for ease of carrying and walked out of his apartment, only to find that passing cars more closely resembled camels and the paved highway a sandy desert. He nearly pinched himself to see if he was dreaming, he was not.

His nylon windbreaker had been replaced by a coarsely woven robe and his box of treasures by a reed basket now filled with papyrus scrolls, ancient writing materials, and two loaves of something resembling artisan bread. There was no sign of the city, his apartment building, nor anything that would indicate where he had recently been or where he now was. Intrigued, and maybe a little apprehensive, he approached and joined the passing caravan without conversation. His Nike sport shoes were gone and, in their place, were crudely made but sturdy leather sandals.

I should mention that Clint was very fluent in both the Greek and Hebrew languages, which was a necessity in doing his job properly. Although there were many dialects, the root meanings and pronunciations of those languages were second nature to him.

"Where are we going?" he asked one of those walking beside him.

"To Egypt of course," the man answered. "To trade goods with the Egyptians."

From the reference Clint determined the probable timeline of the events, which was made even more certain when the caravan stopped and bartered with some men about buying a young slave. The young man seemed to be in his late teens and from a family of station by his demeanor and dress.

After two days travel, the walls of a city embraced them and welcomed them into a square where others like themselves had set up shop and were haggling with the locals over price and quality. Clint disengaged himself from the troupe and took a seat nearby to see how the scene would play out. Goods of all sorts were traded, with the participants speaking more and more loudly as they tried to dominate the conversations and best one another.

Finally, the young slave was brought to center court where interested parties could judge his worth and begin bidding for ownership. The bidding ended when a man of obvious importance outbid his peers and took the young man into his custody. That man, Clint soon learned, was called Potiphar. He was the captain of the palace guard. Clint immediately determined that he was living out a story from the Bible and was determined to record the events as he experienced them first-hand on those scrolls in his possession.

Although he had no idea of why he was there or how long he might stay, he made preparations for the long haul and was soon hired on as guard in the prison. Clint, knowing the Biblical story but not privy to actual events in Potiphar's household, waited and soon, the young man was imprisoned.

"Who are you and why are you here?" Clint asked the young prisoner.

"My name is Joseph," he answered. "I am a Jew from Canaan who was sold into slavery by my brothers and then wrongfully accused of a crime against my master."

"Be strong," Clint advised, without expounding more, "and remain true to your God."

Many days went by with little change in the young man's status, until finally he was joined in his cell by the Pharaoh's baker and wine steward, who had also fallen from favor. In time, they became friends and came to Joseph for help in understanding their dreams. In God's wisdom he told them the meaning of their dreams and in three days his prophecy became true.

Clint watched and waited, knowing the story and it's outcome. As the Bible had said, each part of the story happened just as it was told in scripture. In time, Joseph interpreted the Pharaoh's dream as well and it too happened just as he had said, therefore the King put him Second in Command of all of Egypt. Clint remembered the account in Genesis nearly word for word as the drama continued to unfold. In the end, just as was foretold in the Word of God, Joseph was reunited with his father and his brothers.

Clint was still walking across the parking lot holding his box of valuables when he heard the noises of traffic and was startled to recognize the familiar surroundings. Did it really happen, he asked himself, or was I dreaming? Weeks went by before he opened up his PC and recognized his own account of the incident which had apparently been transferred from the scrolls to the computer supernaturally.

It was evening but because it was summer, the sun was still in the sky. Overhead was a deep azure blue while in the west, fiery shades of red, orange, and yellow proclaimed the glory of God. All at once the backdrop of modern buildings was replaced by crude huts and unfamiliar surroundings. Clint again was dressed much as before and was watching as an old man with dark flowing hair stood staring into the sky, when a booming Voice stated, "I can no longer tolerate man's wickedness, I am going to destroy mankind and the world, only you and your family will be spared."

Clint listened as God went on to describe to Noah exactly how to build the ark and what was expected of him, in words so familiar to the young scholar. He then watched, as time seemed to speed up, while the old man, Shem, Ham, and Japheth built the giant ship and readied it for the flood, which was still yet to come. He listened intently to their conversations and watched and grieved as Noah's neighbors came and went, jeering and refusing his invitation to join them on the ark, just as God had said they would. He was amazed as he carefully and meticulously wrote the story down on the scrolls which had been provided to him. Just as the rain began to fall, he found himself walking across his own back yard, admiring the beautiful sunset.

Weeks went by without incident, but Clint still hesitated to share his experience with anyone, and returned to his normal duties. He must have fallen asleep at his computer because when he awakened, he was outside, standing in an open valley, surrounded by low mountains. A great number of soldiers in military dress were sporting armor and weapons of war and all-around, trumpets blared and a loud voice from the hills boasted, "send down one man to fight me, if I kill him you will be our subjects, if he should prevail, we will serve you."

Clint immediately recognized the incident from his Biblical training and knew the bellowing voice belonged to a giant of a man named Goliath. He had made the same offer several days in a row but did not find a single Jew who would take the challenge. Behind Clint, a commotion got his attention. The diminutive figure of a young man was speaking harshly to King Saul, pleading that someone should champion the God of Israel against the Philistines. Most of the seasoned soldiers scoffed at the boy and his foolish attitude toward challenging the great warrior, but none had the heart to take the challenge themselves.

Clint could smell the sweat of the prancing horses, hear the rustling of swords and clash of shields, and in spite of knowing the outcome of the contest, was drawn into the drama as all waited breathlessly while the small, frail boy was dressed in the king's armor.

There were many more seasoned warriors who had faltered, looking at the giant, who stood almost ten feet tall when dressed in his armor. Brave men who not only feared death but feared they would leave their countrymen in bondage. The king's armor, of course, was an ill fit and its mere weight would have been more than David could bear. When he walked out onto the field, Goliath was twice his height and more than four times his weight. David carried in one hand a shepherd's staff and in the other a leather pouch which was joined by two long leather thongs, and around his waist, in his shepherd's pouch, were five smooth stones.

The giant's laughter, which rang all across the valley, was quickly followed by that of his comrades in arms, who could smell victory in the air. As the gap between them narrowed, the Philistine again roared with laughter at his enemy and spoke harshly to him. David responded in kind and stated that it was not he, but his God, who would claim the victory for His own glory.

Less than a minute later, Goliath lay dead on the ground, with a small stone protruding from his forehead. David took Goliath's own sword and cut off his head, and with that, fulfilled his promise of victory. Clint was energized and felt the Lord's presence as he awakened and saw the incident that had again been written on scrolls, was also clearly written out on his computer screen in his home office.

Days later, the sea was calm when the small wooden vessel left shore and put out from Joppa, headed toward Tarshish, which was far across the Mediterranean Sea. Clint found himself working as a deckhand, a job for which his small stature and physical condition was ill suited. The ship was carrying freight, and required that all passengers were expected to pull their own weight as part of their fare. The crew was made up of many cultures from many lands, each with their own languages and religious beliefs. Clint was amazed, however, how buy-and-large they seemed to blend together into a reasonably efficient labor force, under the tutelage of the Captain and his seasoned crew. The ship was heavily laden with goods stored both under and upon its wooden deck, and rode low in the water, as it bore their considerable weight.

After just two days, the crew had fallen into a routine and new friendships were being made among the men. Clint bunked not far from a small, dark-skinned man who kept himself mostly apart from the rest of the crew and only spoke when spoken to. His name, Clint learned, was Jonah, a rebellious prophet. Excitement filled Clint as he correctly realized the adventure into which he had now been placed.

What an opportunity, he thought, to be privileged to have a first-hand account of one of his favorite Bible stories. The timeline he remembered was approximately 800 BC. Clint was not an outdoorsman, or suited for hard labor or by nature one who sought out adventure, and yet here he was. His thoughts turned to home, his wife, friends, and his job, none of which provided what God, it seemed, was now providing him. He wondered how long this roller coaster would last and why he'd been chosen to ride it. Once again, he took notes.

On the third day he awoke to the sound of thunder and felt the deck pitching and yawing beneath his sandaled feet. When he climbed to the top deck, he could see that dark clouds were blowing in from the shore and the sea was becoming more and more treacherous. Seasoned sailors were running about barking orders to the unskilled crew. The storm continued to worsen throughout the night and by the next morning, the small wooden vessel was in danger of sinking.

The captain was an experienced man who could see they were in peril and ordered the cargo be thrown into the ocean in an effort to keep the ship afloat. That done, the storm continued to worsen and the men questioned why their prayers to their gods for safety was not working, and then wondered who may be responsible for the storm. It was decided that one of them must have sinned. Soon Jonah admitted to them about his sin of trying to flee from God and told them to throw him into the sea. The crew did not hesitate, and over the side he went into the stormy water.

Clint observed that the weight of Jonah's wet woolen robe took him quickly down and out of sight, and just as it did, the water became calm. He remembered the familiar story from the Bible nearly word for word, and pictured in his mind what was happening somewhere deep below the boat. Unknown to the captain and his crew, the Biblical events known to true believers were rapidly taking place.

As he sank, seaweed wound itself around Jonah, leaving him incapacitated, then just before he would have drowned, a fish of huge proportions swallowed him in a single bite.

Clint remembered the prophet was in the belly of the great fish for three days, praying to God for salvation and admitting his sin of unfaithfulness. On the third day after the incident, Clint found himself walking along a sandy beach alone, when suddenly the sea parted and a great fish spit Jonah out of its mouth and onto the shore, right in front of him.

Jonah was a mess, covered with slime and bleached nearly white by the fish's stomach acids, but was quite contrite and focused on getting to Nineveh to spread the word that the city was to be destroyed for its sins. Clint helped him clean up a bit before accompanying him to Nineveh, where the prophet spread the word that was, to his surprise and disappointment, well received.

Something in Jonah seemed to want the full weight of God's judgment to fall on the city rather than have them they repent. Clint considered how modern man wants his enemies to "get what they have coming," almost in the same manner. Before he was spirited away back to the present, he left Jonah lying under the shade of a large leafed plant, hiding from the sun, seemingly still bitter that God has shown mercy on the city. At home, the events of his adventure had again been recorded.

Clinton was antsy, both at work and at home, eagerly seeking a new adventure and when none came, he became disconsolate to the point that others began to notice and comment. He finally confided with his wife the full extent of what had recently happened to him, while fully expecting that she may suggest a visit to the hospital for evaluation. She did not, instead she listened quietly, asking only a few questions for clarification, then smiled and said, "I don't suppose you could invite a companion to go with you next time." Her comment eased the tension he'd felt and helped him return to the mundane tasks at hand.

Just when he'd determined that his field trips into the past were over, he had finished toweling off after his morning shower and dressed, suddenly finding himself standing in the home of Rahab, the prostitute. Several others who had also been sent as spies were there to bring back word to Joshua, the leader of the Israelites, for the purposes of conquering and destroying the Canaanites, which God had ordered.

Biblical history tells us of God's people being freed from slavery in Egypt, wandering in the wilderness for forty years, and finally arriving at the Promised Land. Moses had already handed leadership over to Joshua, son of Nun, and then died and was buried, before the Israelites crossed into Canaan. Word came back with the spies that the Canaanites feared Israel and their God, so their army surrounded the walled city of Jericho.

Each day, the army of God circled the city. Clint observed the height and breadth of the massive walls, which looked for all purposes impenetrable, and marveled at what he knew was about to happen. Six days they marched once around the city silently, on the seventh day they marched around it seven times, before blowing their horns and giving a great shout. The walls fell, as though by an earthquake, allowing the army to climb over the rubble and kill their enemies.

Clint marveled at the accuracy of how the event transpired relevant to how it had been described in the Bible, since many modern scholars questioned if the event was factual. He was, however, aghast at the savagery of the Israelites, who had been instructed to destroy every living thing from the heathen culture so as not to pollute the purity of God's chosen people. Clint stayed with them a few days before being summarily returned to his bathroom, where he finished grooming for work.

As he waited, he wondered what may lie ahead... the story of Daniel in the lion's den, something concerning Moses and the Pharaoh, or possibly the Nazarite strongman Samson, the last of the judges. Instead, his journey began with a walk in uncharted territory, a first-hand account of an event which had taken place during the 400 years of silence between the Old and New Testaments.

"Who are you?" the rough voice questioned. The uniformed man who spoke wore what appeared to be a military uniform with a broadsword hanging heavily from his belt. "Why are you not on your knees?"

Clint hesitated, trying to grasp where he was and how he should answer.

"Who dares to question his superiors in such a coarse manner?" he finally replied, answering a question with a question, while he stalled for time.

The guard answered by knocking Clint from his feet, then said, "bow before Cyrus the Great, you worthless dog."

Clint's mind searched for events in ancient history and determined that he was in the past, sometime between 400 BC and 340 BC. He bowed until his forehead touched the ground and assumed a humble posture, remaining so until Cyrus finally spoke.

"Who are you?" the King demanded, "and how is it you have referred to yourself as our betters?"

"Please forgive my impertinence, master, I am but a traveler from far away and knew not in whose presence I stood," Clint answered contritely, but wondering if he were to be killed here in the past, how it would affect the future.

"I am puzzled," Cyrus continued, while shaking his head in disbelief. "Are you a sorcerer? One moment you were not here and the next you stood before me just as you are."

He thought it wise not to try and explain the seemingly unexplainable so he said simply, "I know not Great King, it was as if I had fallen asleep and when I awakened, I found myself here."

In essence what he had said was true and conveyed his true ignorance of the situation, while leaving the door open to the king's imagination.

"Stand," Cyrus ordered, "while I consider what you have said."

Clint stood and took a breath as the tension in the room seemed to dissipate.

After several minutes, while they waited in silence, Cyrus finally spoke. "Are you a Jew?" he asked.

"My ancestors were Jews," he answered correctly, without trying to expound further upon his lineage.

"By what name are you called?" the King continued.

He thought for a moment before answering, "Clintonious," he said, grasping at a Greek/Roman interpretation to appear more in tune with the period.

"You will join me at my table," the King said graciously. "I have many questions to ask of you, Clintonious."

Clint lowered his eyes, nodded his head, and bowed, thus indicating that he accepted the King's offer. He was quickly ushered to a room where he was given water to bathe himself and fine clothing to replace those which God had provided. As he waited to be summoned, he once again searched his mind for more indications of just where in time he had been placed.

Obviously, Nebuchadnezzar's reign was over and Babylon had been defeated. The Jews were now governed by Persia, but was it before or after the events described in the Bible including the rebuilding of the temple, he did not know. He himself had many questions to ask of his benefactor.

God's Word tells of a time when King Ahaz made an unholy alliance with his enemy, rather than trusting in God and ultimately Jerusalem was destroyed and Israel taken into captivity for her disobedience. Clint knew the timeline and the succession of great rulers and nations which ruled over God's chosen people from his previous studies of Daniel and others of God's prophets. King Cyrus, although a conqueror, was a wise and merciful ruler, much more so than the Babylonians had been. One might easily conclude that God had touched his heart in such a way as to cause him to show favor to the errant nation, whom God had chosen as His own.

At the head of a great table filled with food and delicacies sat the King, surrounded by his noblemen and advisors. An empty seat on his right had been chosen for his new guest, Clintonious. As he entered the great hall, the King waived Clint toward the empty chair and said, "sit and join me."

Overwhelmed by both fear and curiosity, Clint did as he was told. The King was clearly not without intelligence and insight when he asked him many pointed questions, many of which Clint struggled to answer honestly, while withholding the whole truth.

"You are a prophet then?" Cyrus asked. "Your God, Yahweh, is a powerful God who rules mighty nations, even as I rule this nation." It was more of a statement than a question, with which Clint could not take exception. He nodded and smiled at the ruler's insight, wondering as he did, if the true prophets of God may have possibly taken the same sort of journey as he was now taking.

Clint felt drawn to the man, both because of his personality and humor, but also because he knew much about him from past studies. They spoke as friends, almost equals, while others at the table listened, entranced by their dialogue.

"Where then is the "King's cupbearer?" Clint asked, referring of course to Nehemiah.

"He has returned to his homeland to rebuild his God's temple," Cyrus answered. "Do you know him?"

"I know *of* him," Clint answered honestly, "but have yet to meet him."

"Perhaps you will," the King responded. "Do you have insight into such things?"

Clint smiled and shook his head. "Alas, no, I know only of

those things which my God allows."

"How long will I reign?" the King asked offhandedly. "Do you know?"

"I know only that Persia will reign 200 years before it is defeated by another great ruler like yourself," Clint answered, while thinking ahead to the coming time of Alexander the Great.

The King looked distressed by the message. He terminated their conversation and sent his guests, including Clint, away.

Clint was resting uneasily, trying to sleep, when a picture of a robed man holding a knife flashed across his mind. He seemed to be moving stealthily down a long passage with some devious motive in mind. Clint bolted from the mat on the floor and went to the door where a guard stood.

"The King is in danger!" he shouted. "Act quickly!"

The guard ran down the hallway where he recruited others before proceeding toward the King's quarters. There, on the floor lying in his own blood, was the King's personal guard. They rushed into his chamber just in time to slay the intruder and save their King.

Clint could hear shouting and a furor of activity as the soldiers attempted to determine if other assailants posed further danger, but none were found. Within a few minutes he was sum-moned to the King's room, where Cyrus sat waiting for his arrival.

"Did your God reveal the assassin to you?" he demanded. "For what purpose did He choose to save my life?"

"Yes, in a dream," Clint answered. "Why you were spared, I do not know"

"Tell me about your God," Cyrus asked softly, while motioning the soldiers away.

Ironic, Clint thought, that I've traveled centuries back in time to give witness to a pagan king about the coming King. They spent several hours together while Clint told of the future as he knew it, without telling Cyrus how he came by the knowledge which he was sharing. He stopped his dialogue with the book Revelation, seeing no reason to speak about the modern world.

"I will die, but I will not die," Cyrus said, shaking his head while trying to understand. "And if I believe what you say and bow my knee to your God, I'll live forever?"

"Yes," Clint answered simply.

"Let me consider what you have said," the King replied, before dismissing his guest.

Clint awakened suddenly, bathed in sweat, his heart racing, wondering where he was before recognizing the familiar face of his digital clock. He was home in his own bed, unsure if it had been a dream or another trip into the past to serve God's unknown purpose.

At What Price....

You fill in the blank. Everything we value has a price – please consider what you value and what price you are willing to pay for it. The price of some things is hidden in the ***fine print*** so carefully consider what the ***full cost*** may be before you choose. Now please also consider what legal tender is used to make that payment. Often it is a portion of our life or our happiness which we trade for our dreams.

~   ~

Ted was eighteen – handsome, popular, and blessed with many physical and mental gifts – he was both admired and envied by his peers. Unfortunately, he aspired to show the world he had everything, while in his heart he felt he really had nothing.

When his abusive drunken father had finally left them Ted was twelve, his mother had turned first to prescription drugs for relief from the pain of her injuries and then to illegal ones to numb her broken heart and shattered psyche. He had made them both feel small and worthless which, no doubt, gave his own sagging ego a boost. Inexplicably in his young mind, and even knowing his father was really at fault, Ted blamed his mother for the breakup and became rebellious and distant when she needed him the most, which left them both with nothing.

Ted was, by nature, a leader and as such, others seemed to flock to him to provide leadership, which of course he was ill suited to give.

"Come on Ted, let's have some fun," Martin said. "We've got all the candy we can eat."

"Yeah, "Tommy chirped as they walked along the sidewalk, "Let's do some trickin'!"

As you may have already guessed, it was Halloween night and the four sixth-grade boys were feeling their oats.

"Dad told me about a time when he was young, when they used a horse to pull over an outhouse," Billy Martinez added.

"I don't see no outhouses or horses," Ted replied dryly. "We have to think up our own pranks."

"Whatcha thinkin"? Martin asked in a conspiratorial tone.

They continued walking to the end of the block before stopping at the corner of Main and Elm. Main Street was deserted, with only the streetlights and an occasional light in a shop window to illuminate it. The citizenry was all at home as the hour grew close to midnight, and the small burg rolled up its sidewalks for the night.

"Let's go back to my house," Ted suggested in a whisper. "My Dad has a big logging chain in the shop."

'Big' fell short of describing the massive chain, whose links were a half-inch in diameter. It took all three of the boys to carry it and then load it into the trunk of their old Buick Roadmaster.

A quick drive down Main Street confirmed their suspicions. As they backed into a darkened spot between two businesses, they could just make out the silhouette of the old black and white cruiser which the town Sheriff drove.

As always, he was lying in wait for some forgetful citizen to drive through the darkened town above the posted speed of 25 MPH. His contract with the city stipulated he'd get 50% of all fines collected within city limits, as part of his meager salary. They circled the block, parked in the alleyway behind the mercantile and lugged the chain to where the Sheriff was parked, half dozing. One end was fastened to a nearby power pole, the other draped quietly around the rear axle of the car, while leaving considerable slack in it.

Ted smiled mischievously as he climbed behind the wheel waiting for Tommy, Billy, and Martin to join him in the car.

"Ready?" he asked, as the old Buick came to life in a cloud of smoke.

"Ready as we'll ever be!" Martin answered.

They drove south two blocks before turning back onto Main Street, where they cut their lights, and brought the old V8 up to speed. Roaring down Main at 70 they hardly had time to see the Sheriff flip on his lights and start pursuit before his car bucked upward like a two-year-old colt, and came to rest only partly into the street, with no rear axle.

Laughing as only teens can, they returned home and parked the car, then spent the next three hours rehashing the event. The next day the small town was abuzz with variations of what had happened and opinions of who may have done it.

A good story is only good if one can share it and soon news leaked out who was involved. Unknown to them, the Sheriff was in the hospital with a broken back and odds were he'd never walk again. All four boys were sentenced to the youth correctional facility in Cottonwood, Idaho, where they learned that life indeed does have consequences.

The Blind Dog

Pet lover or not, most would agree that there is something special about a dog. A dog is loyal, forgiving, and accepting of mankind's weaknesses. A dog will accept guidance and direction where a cat will not. A dog will lick the hand that has just disciplined him. A dog seems to have inherent knowledge of our needs, moods, and provides a willing ear to listen while we bare our souls. He'll rush to greet us at the door after a hard day at work and accept it when we are not quite ready to lie down on the floor and play with him. Many dogs seem almost human but without the drama that comes with the human race. Picture now if you will, Small Town USA, a rural hamlet nestled in the food belt somewhere where everyone knows everyone else, and where its value system has not yet been overtaken by the modern world.

~   ~

Dot, the mother of the seven mix-breed pups, was a farm dog and as such was an integral part of the family. That she'd wandered off and found a mate surprised no one, for unless restrained, such is the way of nature. Over the next few months, each of the puppies were given away except one – the one about whom this story is written – the family called him Pooch.

Originally there had been seven of them pushing and shoving to get near enough to their mother to feast on her rich milk. Much to little Sarah's disappointment the runt, the smallest and weakest one, was pushed aside by his siblings and only through her compassion and diligence did he survive.

Sarah was the youngest of three sisters, the most sensitive and precocious. Mary and Louise were more practical and had common sense like their mother, who was the typical hardworking farm wife and diligent mate to her husband. It fell to Sarah to care for Pooch, while the older and more responsible sisters helped with chores around the house.

Sarah and Pooch would wander the fields and hills around the farm, while stopping to inspect each flower or take an opportunity to chase a butterfly, without regard to the serious world surrounding them. As she grew and matured, she changed very little, with her vision of the world around her very different than her siblings.

Sarah was a tender-hearted "fixer" by nature, one who would always choose the underdog and champion its cause. That, her parents thought, was why she had chosen to marry Jake. To them he was an unlikely loser who'd never amount to anything, or be independent enough to cut the apron strings that bound him to his mother. Her ex-husband, Jake's father, was much like the adult son whom she was still raising when Sarah took notice of him, and made it her mission in life to help him become more than he currently was. Sarah was sure that as the product of a broken home, and lacking self-esteem and ambition, Jake was just waiting for her to come along and save him.

They married not long after his mother's death, some thought because he now lacked someone to care for him as his mother always had. Sarah, of course, cared not a whit what anyone else thought of Jake or his irresponsible view of life.

They inherited his family home and with it a great deal of maintenance, now long overdue. Sarah got a job at the library which paid little but provided something, and gave her the opportunity to travel the world through reading, which was her passion. Jake had the unique ability to seem busy while not accomplishing anything.

They lived a meager existence, unable neither to maintain or improve their circumstance, nor to even keep current on their property taxes on the pittance her job provided. Eventually, Sarah was forced to face the reality of their situation and demand that Jake find employment. To everyone's surprise, he found his niche as an apprentice welder in a local shop and seemed well-suited to the job, notwithstanding the need to arrive on time and work regular hours.

Pooch was now just over ten years old and was the one luxury Sarah forced them to afford. Although he did not eat much, they had little to share, which forced him to forage for himself. That is how he became a fixture in the small town of their residence. He was laughingly named Pooch the Mooch by the locals, who gave him handouts.

As time went by, the unlikely couple endured and were eventually accepted by the little community. Pooch would follow Jake to work each day, where he would lay and watch his master weld. Five years after they were married, Sarah took ill and died, leaving her husband and an aging dog behind. Without family to anchor him and provide what he was lacking, Jake moved on to parts unknown, leaving both Pooch and the ramshackle house behind for someone else to care for.

He was a fixture in the community for as long as many could remember, most did not know from where he came or where he disappeared to when not quietly prowling the streets or alleys looking for a morsel of food. There was an element of truth to the conjecture among the patrons at the barber shop that he'd once belonged to an iron worker who had died and had become blind from watching as his master ply his trade, while welding steel parts together. There was a blue haze covering both eyes, much the same as one may see with someone who has cataracts. In any event, he could not see at all and depended on the black nose at the end of his graying muzzle and his floppy ears to direct his feet to his next meal.

Unfortunately, he had endured both sticks and stones, harsh words, and even the toe of a boot now and then, as he fought to find food in alleys and trash cans behind homes and businesses throughout the town. He was old – no one knew just how old – but his graying coat and unsteady gait indicated he may be well over a dozen years and possibly nearly twice that.

He instinctively knew which of the shopkeepers could be depended on for a morsel of food, a pat on the head, and a kind word and also which to pass quickly by to avoid a verbal or physical assault. He surely knew how many steps were in a city block and acknowledged when traffic stopped to allow he and pediatricians to cross the street. Without a doubt, he'd been hit more than once by cars hurrying to get through a red light, but had never been seriously injured. Town folks each had their own name for him, which suited him fine. He'd recognize the voice and then pair it with the name they called out. In dog-speak he had a name for each of them, the name they called him by.

He'd lay in the sunshine listening to the familiar sounds of children playing in the school yard or stroll across the park to where the ducks and geese floated easily atop the small pond. He had been known only once to give a menacing growl and that when some stranger tried to take a little girl's hand in the park. She'd squealed and resisted his tug on her hand and was, no doubt, saved by her blind friend who was nearby. The assailant, unknowing of the dog's condition, beat a hasty retreat from the park before police could arrive.

Somehow, with the changing temperature that the summer season brought with it, he sensed that the Fourth of July was not far distant. It was the only time of the year that he truly despised, with the noise and clamor which surrounded it and the unsettling explosions in the sky which he could neither see nor understand. Of course, he had not always been blind, but in dog years it had been more than a quarter of a century since he could make out anything except light and darkness.

"Nice doggie," a young voice said as someone patted his head before their mother had admonished them not to touch him and warned that he probably had fleas.

Some of what he heard he instinctively understood by the tone of the voice and by what action preceded or followed. Harsh voices were a warning of the possibility of injury while softer tones usually were followed with a tasty morsel of someone's lunch.

"Hey Butch, come here," a familiar voice beckoned. "I've got something for you."

He turned toward the direction the voice had called and walked the few steps to the park bench and waited until his nose picked up the smell of greasy deep-fried chicken. He sat and wagged his long tail waiting for further invitation.

"Here boy," the young male voice offered. "Help me finish up this fried chicken."

In that day no one gave a second thought to what sort of food a dog should or should not eat, whether the bones might shatter and do internal damage or not, or if his diet provided just the sort of things touted by commercial manufacturers. Dogs ate what they were offered or not as they chose. The old dog was thinking, *'this is Butch, I know him and have shared his lunch several times'* as he moved closer to the greasy hand holding out what was left of a thigh. He formulated a mental picture of what he thought Butch should look like, had he been able to see him, and liked what he saw. The musical laughter of young children echoed in the back ground as Butch held out his hand with more small pieces of chicken and crispy skin for the dog to enjoy.

"Good boy, Butch," the voice said cheerfully. "Here, clean up my fingers for me."

The old dog was happy to oblige his gracious benefactor.

~   ~

It was late summer and the sun's stifling heat had forced Pooch to find shelter under a tree near the pond in the park. If it was not for the light breeze blowing up the valley, the temperature would surely have been above 100°. Pooch lay just out of the direct rays of the sun, enjoying the coolness of the ground beneath him, he was half asleep, dreaming of Sarah and those days when they had roamed the hills together. Suddenly, just a short distance away, the scream of a child in peril filled his ears and brought him to his feet. To his left, other children seemed also to be screaming and crying out for help, running feet and louder deeper, voices behind him, also the sound of water thrashing far out into the pond, followed by pleas for help.

He did not hesitate as he plunged into the water and swam

toward the splashing sound of the drowning child. In his mind was a clear picture of young Sarah who was pleading for his help. Well over 80 in human years, he never-the-less maintained the determination to save the child.

Unfortunately, the adults on the beach who had gathered were too late to offer practical assistance. He swam on toward the child and just as his strength began to wane, he felt a small hand grasp the long fur on his back and cling to him. The weight of the child nearly pulled him under with her, but then as he turned toward the cheering voices he could feel the child skimming along behind him. He, of course, had no concept of distance and swam on with his heart now beating wildly in his chest, until his feet touched ground in the shallow water. Eager hands took charge of the child, turning their attention away from Pooch.

Walking unsteadily away from the clamor of the crowd, he laid down under the same tree from where he had come. The next thing he saw was bright lights and colors as he had seen as a pup. Some say there's a doggie heaven and if true, Pooch lives there.

The Old Soldier

Much like the first snowflake of winter, the old soldier finally fell,
As with all before him, Death had cast its spell.
For eighty years and more, his great heart ne'er missed a beat,
But now still and lifeless, he lay at his Master's feet.

"You've done well," the Master said,
Now stroking the thin white hair on his head.
The old man's eyes opened and a smile filled his face,
"Dare I ask," he said smiling. "What do you call this place?"

His smile became contagious as his Master did the same,
"We call it home," He answered, "but Heaven is its name."
"And you, you must be Jesus," the soldier said with glee,
"The Son of God Almighty, the One who died for me!"

His dark eyes were a twinkle as He looked down on His son,
"I knew the day you were born," He said, "you'd be a special one."
Tears rimmed the old man's eyes, deep-set in his wrinkled face,
Quietly he answered, "Special maybe, but not enough that You
should take my place."

Jesus answered, "My love is without measure,
As it must always be."
"It was My choice to die for all,
Who give their lives to Me."

The Noble Assassin

Doug (Ace) Browning was hardly on a par with the famed Chris Kyle, but possibly would have someday been if fate had not called him to a different purpose. He'd grown up on a small quarter section farm in Gooding, Idaho, which had once belonged to his grandfather and now to his father. A third generation Idahoan and patriot, he'd nearly cut his teeth on the old .22 Winchester pump with an octagon barrel, which that same grandfather had passed down to him. By age six he no longer cared to shoot the large fat groundhogs that lived in the remains of the lava beds which bordered most of their fertile rich farm fields. The **hogs**, some weighing upwards of twenty pounds, loved to eat the alfalfa and row crops and did so with only hawks, eagles, and coyotes as their natural predators. Doug and his father would often take time from their regular chores to help keep nature in balance without totally eradicating the sleek fat rodents.

However, as his skills grew, Doug tired of shooting the easy targets and sought out harder prey. Ground squirrels, also called "picket pins" by many, weighed less than a half pound and stood only two or sometimes three inches tall when fully grown. A head shot would be like shooting a nickel at a hundred yards which took surprising skill with iron sights. Grandpa Browning, a quiet, smallish man, had been an infantryman who served with pride in

Europe during the Second World War. His dress uniform, which still hung in the back of the closet, had on it many service ribbons which had caught Doug's eye early in his life, but about which he had received very little information from the aging man. Only after his death had his own father recounted stories of the feats of heroism and bravery that had caused them to be presented to the humble farm boy from the potato state.

Doug's father, a Korean War veteran, was like his father, similarly close mouthed about his time spent across the Pacific Ocean fighting against enemies of democracy. It seems true heroes are often so, they see nothing special about themselves about which to brag, but rather, leaving others to tell stories of their heroism.

George Bush had been replaced as president and Barak Obama had just taken office in the White House. The events of 911 were still fresh on America's mind, when Doug and a quarter of his graduating class joined the military. With right hands raised, they made lifetime promises to "protect and defend their nation against all enemies both foreign and domestic." Those words struck a chord in his heart, knowing that this promise was one that didn't end, even when his service was completed.

Doug (Ace) received his nick-name while in basic training on the firing range, where on a bet, he obliterated all of the black from an ace-of-spades at two hundred yards with five successive rounds from his service rifle. His prowess did not go unnoticed by his superiors, who summarily cut orders which placed him in sniper school. Three years later, Ace found himself in the Middle East in harms way, doing just what God had equipped him to do.

His spotter, just a few feet away, was lying prone glassing the remains of bombed out structures that others of their team were progressing toward in an effort to ferret out any remaining ISIS militants. Likewise, Ace used his scope to evaluate apparent movements or suspicious shapes in the smoking rubble. Doug found it difficult to rationalize the mindset of the enemy who had no qualms about torturing or killing innocents for the sake of their false god.

Just prior to closing his hand and feathering the trigger, his mind always prayed the same prayer, "God, please allow me to make this shot but only as Your will determines." Try as he must, he had lain awake many nights wondering if God was sharing His own pain with him in that one of His own children had to die. He always felt something akin to pain when his bullet found its mark.

"I have movement one klick out just under the lower right window," his spotter whispered.

Ace moved his weapon, adjusted his range finder and immediately saw what his friend had just described.

"A dog," he said laughing. "If he hangs around too long he'll find himself in some rag head's dinner pot."

Doug observed that the dog seemed to be moving across the rubble in a more or less organized manner, much the same as his own bird dog would have done back home while searching a stubble field for pheasants.

"He's looking for something," Ace said, while keeping a sharp eye on the dog and the area behind it.

"He's a mine sweep," the spotter suggested. "He's looking for explosives."

Ace nodded imperceptibly before adjusting his scope once more, to enlarge the picture of the area behind the rubble and under a vacant window opening, just over a half mile away. The minimal breeze occasionally lifted a piece of poorly tied black turban just above the rubble.

"You see it?" Ace asked Jake. "It looks like a loose piece of black fabric to the left side and behind the dog."

"You got some eyes man," Jake answered snickering. "Maybe it's just some dead guy's clothes or something."

"You see that?" Ace asked again with enthusiasm. "I just saw the sun reflect off something. I think someone is glassing us, stay down."

The round arrived a split second before the sound, with the bullet ricocheting off a rock just inches to Jakes right.

Ace turned to see Jake smiling. "I owe you," he said, grinning.

Doug didn't answer, his focus was on the small round object which had given away the sniper's position. His fingers gradually tightened around the grip, as he forced himself to breathe slowly and naturally, he touched the set trigger gingerly while he waited.

Seconds later, he could have sworn he could see his opponent's eye in the lens of his scope as he felt the recoil of his rifle. The absence of the black turban waving in the wind told them what they needed to know. The old dog jumped straight up before then retreating behind the rubble.

"He's down!" Jake announced triumphantly. "Nice shot!"

The familiar pain which always followed a successful kill returned to his chest as he gave his friend a half-smile and nodded silently.

This mission was, as were most others, a success, with all members of their squad returning without injuries. Overhead drones, high flying planes, and satellites with telescopic cameras allowed headquarters a strategic edge over their more primitive enemies. In spite of the technological advantages, many good men still returned home injured or in flag-draped coffins.

They were assembled for the morning briefing when the

Captain said, "Ace, I'd like you and your crew to do a sweep of quad d-12 and make sure we have full control of Hazzad before the main body of ground troops move in."

The request/order was not unusual in itself, only that he'd directly addressed Ace to lead it. For the most part, the chain of command would work through his lieutenant who would then give the order for their squad to take the point and make sure insurgents had been eliminated, to minimize casualties to the larger force. The enemy rarely fought fair, usually they coerced the local population into wearing explosive vests into the proximity of the largest group of Americans, where it was then detonated. Human life seemed to hold little value to them, which put the American forces at a disadvantage.

They were only two klicks from their target when their Humvee seemed to lift high into the air, like a bucking bronc trying to unseat its rider, only then to return to earth and roll on its side, partially on fire. Inside of the twisted metal Ace could see the lifeless remains of three of his friends, including Jake. He attempted to move but found his legs pinned between the floor and the dash. Unknown to him, the rest of his squad which were following behind in a second Humvee had witnessed the explosion and were now hustling toward him.

"Hold on!" a man said into his deaf and bleeding ears. "We'll get you out!"

Many weeks later, he awakened in a bed in Frankfurt, Germany where he had been taken for emergency surgery after first being stabilized at the field hospital.

"He's awake," a young nurse announced to her coworkers with a smile as she walked into his room. She was soon joined by a doctor and several others.

A middle-aged man with oak leaf clusters on his shoulders followed her into the room. "So, Sergeant Browning, you are back with us, are you?" he said smiling. "Can you tell me your name, rank and serial number?"

Ace rattled off the required information, just as if he'd never been injured.

"Very good, now can you give me your parent's names and the town you where you were born?" he continued.

Once again Doug did so, with seemingly little effort.

"What is the last thing you remember before waking up here?" the Colonel asked.

This time, however, he seemed to be having difficulty recalling the incident that had brought him there.

"Hazzad..." he began tentatively, "our mission was in Hazzad."

Suddenly his eyes opened widely and his face changed completely. "My God, my squad... are they alive?" he asked excitedly.

The Colonel shook his head solemnly and answered, "the others in your vehicle did not make it, but those who were following in the vehicle behind are fine. They are the reason you are still alive and with us here today."

Doug's eyes stared at his superior uncomprehendingly.

The officer spoke softly, "it was a sort of miracle, the concussion of the explosion buckled the floor which pushed your legs into the dash. The bleeding was stopped by the pressure of the metal against your wounds or you would surely have bled to death before they could have gotten help."

For the first time, Doug looked down toward the foot of the bed. The rise of the blankets caused by his body stopped about a foot below his waist. The sudden realization that both legs were gone flooded over him like an avalanche. He began to cry.

"You should have let me die," he whispered accusingly. "I should have died with my men."

The doctor nodded to the nurse, who then emptied a syringe into the IV that was attached to the bottle hanging above the wounded soldier. Within seconds his eyes closed and he drifted off to sleep.

"Schedule an MRI," the doctor ordered. "We need to evaluate what, if any, brain damage he may have." The nurse nodded before turning and leaving the room.

Doug's parents had initially been discouraged from flying immediately to Germany after they had received the news of his injury because he was comatose. The call following his awakening sent them scurrying to make travel arrangements. They, of course, had been made aware of the necessity of the amputation and were determined to support their son while he came to grips with the knowledge that his life had been forever changed. Three days later they were shown to his room, looking old and tired after their long trip. Ace was sitting in a wheelchair beside his bed staring blankly out the window.

"Son," his dad said simply, as they walked toward him.

He turned his chair and accepted his mother's embrace and his father's hand, with tears in his eyes. They visited superficially, with no one wanting to speak about his missing limbs.

In an effort to avoid the subject his dad said, "the doctors tell us you are being transferred stateside to Walter Reed, where you'll get therapy." He wanted to bite his tongue when he saw anger appear in his son's eyes before Doug answered bitterly, "yeah, they told me they would fit me with new legs and teach me how to walk."

Doug saw both parents' shoulders drop under the load he

had just given them, and noted the lost look in their tear-filled eyes that now caused him to say, "I'm feeling sorry for myself, I guess I should be grateful for the gift of life God gave me rather than whining about the legs."

Six days later, appearing hale and hearty but still unable to stand or walk, he left on a flight to Walter Reed, with his parents by his side. Silently Doug questioned his faith, God's motives, and the seeming unfairness of his situation. He was a Christian and had always tried hard to follow the guidance of the quiet little voice that he thought was God's Spirit, and yet here he was, a cripple who had let his comrades die. Angry maybe, but not sure if he was angry at God, Americas' enemies, or the damaged body in which he now seemed to be trapped.

Walter Reed Hospital, having been through similar situations thousands of times, knew just what was needed, not only physically but also emotionally, to make the young soldier whole again. To the staff's credit, they seemed to know just when and how hard to push and when to withdraw and let both the body and spirit rest. It took a full six months before Doug walked out of the facility feeling up to the challenge to live what life he had left. Back on the farm in Idaho however, with no therapists or doctors to push him, he became reserved and withdrawn, with little interest in anything but watching the depressing news events on television.

Feeling at loose ends with his new life and without direction he began shooting again, honing his skills and revisiting the pleasure a well-placed shot still gave him. First paper targets, then his favorite targets, the small ground squirrels. Soon however, it was not the old Winchester but a heavy barreled match grade rifle with the best scope he could buy that went with him into the field. As the distance increased his commitment to excellence multiplied also. He was now deadly at six hundred yards, shooting targets the size of a golf ball, but still he practiced.

Doug had been out of the service three years and was still living with his parents when on 9-11-2012, extremists attacked the American consulate in Benghazi, Libya and killed four Americans. The President and leaders in Washington, who could have prevented the attack with nearby forces, instead choose to shut down the proposed rescue operation and demoted the General who had ignored their orders. In his anger, Doug no longer questioned why God had spared him or for what purpose he'd been chosen. He knew the abilities which God had given him were but tools to bring justice to a country in turmoil.

"I'm going back to Walter Reed," Doug told his parents a few days later, while intentionally misrepresenting the reason for his return to the east coast.

"We'll go with you," his mother replied, with concern in her voice. "Is there a problem with your legs?"

"No need," he laughed. "Save your money, I just think maybe they need to give them a tune up, after all, it has been three years since I last visited the VA."

"But, Boise..." she continued. "They have a good hospital there and it's only a day's drive."

"I'm leaving tomorrow," Doug said flatly, putting an end to the conversation.

"Are you okay son?" his father asked putting down his newspaper, with a look of concern on his face.

"Fine Dad," Doug answered, smiling. "Better than I have been in a long time. I just need to get away for a few days and see where I go from here"

Doug flew out of Boise the following morning, stopping in

Denver and then Chicago, before landing at Dulles. He rented a motel room, a car, bought a city map and a newspaper and settled in for the night. He spent the next two days reading and studying what the locals had to say about their President and his Secretary of State and the furor which surrounded the recent Benghazi event. The Democrats tried to defend the indefensible and to sweep the loss of lives under the carpet, while the opposing Republican Party seemed to air new revelations concerning the event each day, but to no avail.

After some negotiation, Doug was able to acquire a short-term lease on an apartment located on the fourth floor, roughly a mile from the White House and within a few minutes of Walter Reed Medical Hospital. In his rented car, he made a quick trip to the first before keeping an appointment at the hospital to have his legs looked at. Afterward, he called home and assured his parents he was safe and things were going well, but he was planning to stay a while longer.

No one seemed to notice the man in 4B or took time to try and know him as a person, as is the way of many on the east coast. Mind your own business, stay to yourself, and don't get involved seemed to be the common theme among the locals.

He kept his second appointment at the hospital where he met Max, his physical therapist, had his prosthesis adjusted and tweaked to work more efficiently, before returning to his apartment. Doug sat on his little deck which overlooked the street below. The landing pad for Marine One was easily visible to the naked eye, as were the ever-vigilant secret service men on the premises at the White House. Doug watched the many flags flying and paid special attention to the direction of the wind at various hours of the day. He made notes as to their estimated speeds and the effect the various tall buildings played in their changing directions.

The little round patio table that was flanked by two inexpensive wrought iron chairs nearly filled the small deck that was accessed from his living area by sliding glass doors. His apartment was small but functional, lacking anything that may have been considered more than the minimum required for a comfortable short-term residence. Ace guessed correctly that it had regularly provided living space for many servicemen like himself, their families, and tourists who needed more than what nearby hotels had to offer.

He developed a routine and by the end of the first week, when he called home, had decided where he thought his future may lead.

"Yeah, things are going fine here, how are you doing?" Doug asked his mother.

"No, not sure yet," he answered his mother's question as to when he might return home. "Say Hi to Dad," he added, before disconnecting.

On the nightstand beside his bed was his well-worn Bible with a dozen bookmarks sticking out of it, and some history books he'd borrowed from the library at Walter Reed. During the day he'd walk and enjoy the fall weather, with its crisp mornings and changing colors, then later he would retire to his apartment and read until drifting off to sleep. Few men, he reasoned, were given opportunity to change the world and then only they whom God had chosen for that purpose. He thought of Judas, the betrayer, who had been created and groomed for the sinister purpose of betraying Jesus, and how unfairly historians seemed to treat him. Could he, should he, have used his free will to do other than what he'd been chosen to do?

A tall, thin, dark-skinned man was escorted regularly from the sanctity of the White House to the waiting helicopter by an entourage of men in dark suits. He was often in the company of a manly-appearing woman of nearly equal height, and by several others whose faces were familiar to anyone watching the evening news. His 50X binoculars, with their range finder lenses, set the distance at 1626 meters, or just over a mile. And, had he been a lip reader, he could have easily listened in on their conversations while sitting in his chair on the deck.

On the White House roof, as many as a dozen secret service men were visible at any given time and could be seen coming and going while changing shifts. Men, he supposed, much like himself, with binoculars, ever vigilant, who had pledged their lives to their country, their only duty was to protect the sitting President.

As Doug thought back to his time in Iraq, he could not remember a single instance where he had held malice toward his intended target... until now. This man, who had surrounded himself with those, who like himself, seemed determined to destroy the very country which he now led. How will history view me, Doug asked himself, and my family. Will they also pay a high price for what I am going to do?

He often prayed a prayer reminiscent of the one prayed so very long ago by Jesus in the garden…. "Father, if there is any other way…" But, much like Jesus, Doug thought he knew the answer before he asked the question.

His carry-on had held nothing except his Bible and his binoculars, the rest of his baggage had been checked in and had ridden across the country without incident, including the parts from his disassembled 300 Winchester Mag and scope. As he Googled sporting goods stores and wrote down several nearby locations, he made a mental list of those components he'd need to buy to reload his own ammunition.

The man looked at him strangely then smiled and answered, "shotgun, pistol, or long rifle?"

"I have all three," Doug answered honestly," but right now I'm thinking of rifle ammo."

"You're military?" the clerk asked off-handedly.

"Yeah," Doug answered, lifting his fatigues to show his artificial limbs. "I'm out here getting therapy at Walter Reed but what I really need is to cuddle up close to my weapon and fire a few rounds. Seems like the folks out here think they can all sit back and sing Kumbaya."

"I know what you mean," the young man answered. "They want it all without having to commit to anything to get it. Thank you for your service. Where are you from?"

"Idaho," Doug answered proudly, "a little town you've never heard of."

"The potato state," the man said smiling. "I know it. Tell me more about yourself."

Doug smiled to himself, picturing his home, but a little tickle had started somewhere in the back of his head that had brought him to question why this man was so interested in him. His sense of danger was something he'd always listened to and had avoided injury or death many times because of it as a soldier in the field.

He looked at his watch and in pretended urgency said, "Oh sorry, I gotta go, I have PT at the hospital in a few minutes. Just give me a box of primers, a pound of Herters 4150, some 165 grain Sierra boat tails, the scales, and the press."

The clerk efficiently put together Doug's order and then asked, "credit or debit?"

Again, the little tickle warned Doug. "Cash," he answered, wanting to retain anonymity.

Doug carefully pulled three $100's out of his wallet with his fingertips and laid them on the counter while thinking maybe he was being overly suspicious.

But when the clerk gave him an insincere smile and asked Doug's name and phone number, he knew better.

"Gotta go," he answered apologetically, while scooping up his merchandise. "We'll visit when I have more time."

Rather than returning to his waiting rental car, he walked briskly across the street and forced himself to have a cup of coffee and a sweet roll, while he waited for his heartbeat to calm. Cameras, he knew, were everywhere, and the right person or agency could easily access them and use facial recognition software to identify him if they wanted. Paranoia, he thought to himself, you are making yourself crazy trying to live in a world for which you have not been trained, and you've watched too many Jason Bourne movies.

He left his car parked and took a taxi toward his apartment but got out a block shy of his destination. Late that evening, he returned, again by taxi, and retrieved the car.

If this is going to happen it must happen soon, he thought to himself as he sat at the small kitchen table while carefully but expertly loading his ammunition.

The PT at Reed smiled as Doug walked into the exercise area and greeted him warmly. "Well sergeant, how are you this fine morning?"

"Fine Max, I'm feeling better every day," he answered. "How about you?"

"Great, thanks for asking. I spent last weekend with my Dad

in Aberdeen at the range," Max replied.

"Your Dad's in the service?" Doug questioned. "What branch?"

"Army. He's a Colonel working at the Pentagon," Tom replied. "Was a Ranger back in the day."

Doug smiled and answered, "once a Ranger, always a Ranger."

"Do you shoot?" the therapist asked.

"I've been known to," Ace answered evasively. "Why do you ask?"

"I just thought you may enjoy a day at the range, they've got an underground tunnel a mile long," the young man said, with enthusiasm.

"I'd love to, but you better check with your Dad first, he'd know the rules about bringing an outsider to the range," Doug suggested.

"It's strange," the PT said looking squarely at Doug. "They caution us to not get close to our patients, but somehow I feel like I have known you all of my life."

Doug smiled but said nothing.

"How old are you?" he asked his patient.

"I turned twenty-six in August," he answered.

"No.... you are kidding me, what day?" the therapist asked.

"10th," Doug replied, knowing his medical records had the same date in them.

The PT literally stopped what he was doing, smiled broadly and then announced, "we're twins from different families. We were born the same day."

To prove his point, he took out his military ID which confirmed what he had just said. "You'll have to meet Dad now for sure, and he'll never believe how this has all come together, what are the odds?"

"Call me," Doug said later as he left the exercise area, wondering what had just happened.

It was a week later, a cold fall morning that had brought with it the first frost, when Doug's cell rang and a familiar voice began speaking to him.

"It's all set. We can drive up Saturday and spend the day on the range, Dad has arranged to provide rifles and ammunition for us!" his new friend said enthusiastically.

"Can I bring my own rifle?" Doug asked. "Hunting season just began last week at home and I hope to get home to do a little elk hunting. I need to sight it in."

"I'll ask," he promised, "and call you right back."

Doug was grateful that he'd been asked no questions about how and where the rifle and ammunition had come from.

"Bring it along," Max advised. "They'll record and mark it at the front gate."

A tall, slender, graying man with a noticeable presence about him walked toward the younger men, smiling before taking his son's hand and then giving him a hug. He then turned to Doug and declared, "Sergeant Douglas Browning I believe," he said, holding out his hand. "I think we may have served together."

Doug resisted the urge to come to attention and salute his superior, and took the offered hand, and then replied, "that is possible sir, although I do not know when or where it may have been."

"Iraq, four years ago. My troops were doing clean up near Hazzad and you and your spotter were making sure any insurgents that were left had been neutralized," the Colonel explained. "I took a few minutes to check up on you before bringing you to the range."

He smiled, turned to his son and then said, "we both may very well take a lesson today in how to shoot a rifle."

The day went well. Doug enjoyed every minute of it and was able to slowly refine his groups of three until they could be covered by a quarter. His sponsor and son watched in wonder as he used his skills. Afterward, the men enjoyed dinner together at the officer's club, with a promise to repeat the outing again before they headed toward DC in separate vehicles.

Doug had pulled the table and chair from the patio back into the room, closed the curtains, while leaving a small opening for the muzzle of his Winchester with its scope to use, turned off the lights, and waited as the rotor wash of the helicopter blades announced their arrival at the White House. He settled comfortably in behind the big gun, adjusted the bipods attached to the fore stock, and closed bolt on a live round and waited. Within minutes, men in dark suits led a trio from the residence, which was then followed by the *preferred press* with their cameras, and yet another contingent of security at the rear.

Doug had watched the familiar parade on television many times, knowing how the events would unfold. The President, who loved seeing himself in the news, would always stop at the foot of the stairs leading into the waiting helicopter, turn back toward the cameras, and give the adoring press a photo-op before boarding.

Ace checked the flags, estimated the wind velocity, and fine tuned the rifle scope until he could see the detail of the man's ear crystal clearly. As expected, the President stopped just as Doug slid his finger into the trigger guard, pushed the safety off, and closed his hand over the grip, while saying his usual prayer. Rather than a loud report and the recoil of the powerful rifle into his shoulder, a metallic click issued from the gun, as he pulled the trigger – a misfire.

For several seconds, he sat unbelieving at what had just

happened before clearly hearing, "This man shall not die at your hand nor at the hand of another, for he is My chosen instrument of retribution upon this nation which I have favored but has now turned her back upon Me," said the commanding voice echoing in Doug's ears. It then continued in a softer tone, "you have served Me well, take heart, you have more work to do still."

Late that night, Doug had been sleeping soundly when he awakened with a Bible verse playing over and over in his head. Genesis 6:11-13 told about God's disappointment at how evil mankind had become and of His decision to destroy everything in a great Flood. Another followed, which told of the people of Israel who had drifted away from God and were then taken into captivity by the Assyrians. He suddenly knew what would happen to America and why nothing or no one could change its fate.

When he landed in Boise the next evening, he knew what he had been called to do... simply live out the Great Commission and guide as many as God calls to salvation.

Three Faces in the Mirror

The face we see peering back at us from our mirror is seldom the same face others see when they look at us. Be it older, younger, more handsome, or less so, the features which identify us are often interpreted differently by our mind's eye. Often, circumstance or emotion plays a part in **what and who** we see when our eye sends a signal to our brain and our brain stores that signal for future use. Two young men or women can look at the opposite sex and arrive at very different conclusions. Perception is an interesting word that describes the blend of what is seen and what appears to be seen. Our story lends insight into what a young woman saw in her mate and into possibly what she should have seen that she did not.

~   ~

"Tim," she said as she closed the door behind her. "I'm home."
No sound answered her.

"Honey, I'm home" she announced, as she sat down her purse, a bag of groceries, and what was left of her lunch on the kitchen counter.

Once again, no reply, no television blaring from the living room, no footsteps coming down the hallway from the bedroom or bathroom, nothing. Instantly, fear gripped her – he was always home by this time, maybe he was in the back yard with his feet up enjoying a beer. She slid open the door and gazed out onto the patio and seeing nothing, walked to the bedroom, bath, and finally into the study, but without success. She immediately dialed his number on the cell and waited until the hollow sounding voice announced a directive to leave a message. With frustration obvious in her voice, she did so before sitting on the couch to wait.

When Kate awakened, it was after 8:00 and a quick glance at her phone confirmed she'd received no calls. Her contact list contained the name and number of her husband's employer, whom she quickly dialed. The **hello** sounded a bit irritated and she could hear a football game playing in the background.

"I told you not to call me at home!" a man's voice said a little too loudly. "You are finished, go find yourself a new job."

Kate hadn't been able to speak or ask the question about where her husband may be, but he obviously was not on the job, so she disconnected without saying a word. Okay, she thought to herself, he'd been fired as he had been by the TSA, and was probably down at the watering hole telling all of his drinking buddies why he'd been let go again without cause. She knew it would do no good to call because whoever answered would look across the bar at the person in question, get the shake of the head and answer, "no I haven't seen him today."

She put on her light jacket and drove the half mile to the corner bar, searching for her husband's pickup as she did, but saw nothing. Inside, raucous laborers were enjoying the company of the close-knit group, each trying to out-shout or out-lie the other, causing pandemonium that made it difficult for the bartender to answer questions. She left, feeling confident that her husband had not been in the establishment that particular day, but with an ever-increasing sense of anxiety concerning his disappearance.

As she drove home, she searched her memory in an effort to remember the events of the preceding day. They had fought, nothing unusual in that, they always seemed to be at each other about something lately, but nothing beyond what she considered "their" normal. It kept coming back to the one-sided phone call she had with his boss, and why he had not called or left a message on her cell about it, or why he was still not at home.

When Kate arrived, the house was dark and foreboding, almost sinister in its stark appearance. An involuntary shiver shook her as she parked her car inside the garage and stepped out of the little compact she affectionately called 'Tess'. She and Tess had been together since high school and over the years had shared many things, both good and bad – her intuition told her this was bad. She contemplated the string of events which had brought her and Tim together and the subsequent changes of location and occupations that had happened in the short three years of their marriage.

Kate had first gone to sleep on the sofa before finally going to bed. When she awakened, the digital clock on the nightstand read 3:26 and there was still no sign of Tim. She had laid awake for what seemed hours when she finally awakened a second time to sound of her doorbell. The clock read 7:14 as Kate pulled on her robe and slippers, before looking out of the peep hole in the front door and seeing a blue uniform with a badge on it.

"Mrs. Roberts?" a strong authoritative voice queried. "Is your husband at home?"

"Yes, I'm Kate Roberts," she answered, feeling a sharp sense of dread in her chest. "No, Tim did not come home last night."

The two men in blue uniforms looked at each other momentarily before asking, "may we come in?"

She welcomed them into the living room and offered them a seat, then went into the kitchen and turned on the coffee pot.

"Coffee will be ready in a few minutes," Kate said as she took a seat across from the two men. "Why are you here?" she asked, a little too bluntly.

She noted that both men were holding a pad of paper on which they were making notes when they answered her question. Tim's truck had been found parked in a darkened corner of the Wal-Mart parking lot by store security, with the driver's side window broken and what appeared to be blood on the seat inside.

Kate gasped. The officer continued that all indications were that someone must have been injured before leaving the scene. Nothing on the store's surveillance cameras was of any value to them because of where his vehicle had been parked. When the officers left, they gave her their business cards and advised that detectives would be in touch with her. Kate closed the door, leaned heavily against it and began to cry, while feeling guilty for what she had been thinking about her husband earlier in the evening.

It was true that Tim had seemed withdrawn and less and less committed to their marriage since they had moved from the east coast and had began his career with the TSA. He seemed more serious and less carefree than when they had first met at a little coffee shop in DC. She had been finishing up her senior year at the university and he, four years her senior, seemed to have a good job with Homeland Security. The transfer to the TSA in Albuquerque, New Mexico had seemed abrupt and unexpected but had appeared to her as a sidewise career move.

However, his sudden layoff a short time later, which forced

him to take a job as a truck driver, had made her question his work ethic and ability to hold a long-term job. At 25, her expectation had been that they'd be living in their own home and making plans to start a family.

"Mom," Kate began as her mother answered the phone, "something may have happened to Tim. He didn't come home last night and the police have found his pickup abandoned."

Her mother gasped and Kate could picture her clutching the front of her robe while she tried to absorb what she was hearing. Kate had intentionally not included the information about the broken car window and the apparent blood stains.

"Your father and I will pray for him right now and then put it out to our prayer chain and ask them pray for his safety," she advised. "Have faith, he'll show up and you'll have good laugh over it someday with your kids."

Her mother's optimism gave Kate's spirits a much-needed momentary lift that allowed her to focus on showering, dressing, and fixing herself a bite of breakfast before she slumped back into worry mode. At 2:00 p.m. there was a knock on the door and two men in business attire stood on the front step. Both held up gold police shields and identification badges, identified themselves as detectives, and asked if they might come in. Kate led them inside, seated them where their colleagues had sat earlier, and joined them.

"We are here to do follow up on your husband's abandoned vehicle," the older of the two stated. "You haven't heard anything from him, have you?"

"No," Kate answered, while tears formed in her blue eyes. "What can I do to help you find him?"

The detective looked down at a note pad he was holding and said, "do you have a current picture of him that we can have, and something with his DNA on it, perhaps a tooth brush or a comb, and a description of what he was wearing when he left for work?"

Kate left the room for a few minutes and returned with his obsolete government ID and a tooth brush in a plastic container. "He was wearing jeans, a white striped short-sleeved cowboy style shirt, Reboks, and a ball cap with his company logo on it," she answered accurately.

The detective looked puzzled and asked, "this says he works for Homeland Security and yet you describe him as though he worked on a ranch."

"I'm sorry," she said, "that ID is a couple of years old but is the most current picture I have of him, he now works, or worked for Southwest Trucking since being let go from the TSA."

"Worked?" the second man asked. "You are saying he does not work there now?"

"When he did not come home last night, I called his boss, who indicated that he'd been fired," she answered.

The two detectives looked at each other quizzically before the lead investigator remarked, "did he say why?"

"No," she answered. "We didn't really talk, he just mostly yelled into his phone probably thinking that it was Tim who was calling him."

"It's safe to say then, that they did not part on good terms?" the detective said. "I'll need his employer's name and the address of his place of business if you have them."

Kate left the room and came back with a paystub in her hand. "His name is Sanders, I think, Ben Sanders. I have his cell phone number right here," she added, as she showed them the contact list on her cell.

Something seemed to be troubling the detective so Kate

finally asked, "is there something more?"

"The job thing, "the other detective answered for him, "normally someone in government service never quits, or transfers, or gets fired. It is unusual to say the least, that he was shuffled from job to job and then was fired from the last two. Do you have a name or number for his supervisor at TSA?"

"Yes, I do," she said. "Tom Bridges and his wife were close friends of ours, and they even came to our wedding."

Once again, her contact list showed both business and home numbers for Tom Bridges.

"Just one more thing and we'll be on our way. Would you object to our looking through Tim's personal things?" he asked.

First distrust, then fear showed in her eyes before she reluctantly nodded and led them to his desk, before leaving the room. The detectives spent better part of an hour looking through the various drawers, papers, and files in the office before rejoining Kate in the living room.

"Is there another place that your husband keeps his personal papers?" the senior man asked.

Kate led them to the closet in the master bedroom where there were several storage boxes that had accompanied them from their apartment in DC to their current one, none of which she had ever opened.

"I haven't any idea what is in them," she stated. "I've had no reason to open them."

Again, she left the room and took a seat on the sofa where she sipped an Earl Grey and waited. It was nearly another hour before they joined her, carrying two of the several boxes with them.

"With your permission, we'd like to take these back to the office and go through them more carefully," the lead detective said.

"Find something?" she asked, her tired voice lacking emotion.

"Can't say," he answered evasively, "but there are things here which may warrant a closer look."

After the detectives left, Kate opened a can of Campbell's soup, poured it in a sauce pan, turned it on low, and opened the day's mail. Nothing but bills and advertisements caught her eye so she settled onto the sofa and turned on the evening news.

Violence, protests, shootings, and bickering over seemingly unsolvable issues like immigration, welfare, and rights for nearly anything someone would want without working for them headlined, as they had for several months. She turned off the tube and closed her eyes, while praying softly for Tim's safety and for the entire crazy world which seemed on the very brink of destruction.

When she awakened, it was dark outside and the soup had boiled dry, ruining the saucepan. The house, even with the lights on, seemed dark and empty and all too quiet.

Two more days passed with no communication from the police, and nothing of course from her husband. Friday morning, as she was dressing to leave for work, the phone rang, it was the FBI.

The man identified himself and explained that they would like to speak with her in person about the disappearance of her husband. He also explained that they had been notified about his disappearance by the local detectives and would now be taking the lead in the investigation. When Kate left for work, her mind was filled with fear as well as a thousand questions all seemingly without answers.

She prayed, with tears running down her cheeks, as she drove woodenly the few miles to her place of employment. A black SUV with government plates was parked at the curb, with two men inside. As she approached, both men got out and stood waiting for her.

The first, a tall, athletic-looking man who was beginning to show grey at his temples stepped toward her, smiled and said, "I'm John Rott, we spoke on the phone, and this is Special Agent Larry Short." Both men were displaying their badges and identification as agent Rott continued. "We've already spoken to your employer, who has agreed to allow us the use of your conference room."

Kate was relieved that she'd not have to be the one to ask for time off since until now, she had not shared the news of her husband's disappearance with anyone. Mr. White, a no-nonsense man and senior partner, was in his seventies and expected his crew to work as hard as he still did. Due to the booming housing market in the area, the little title company was working 10-hour days, six days a week and just holding its own. To allow a key employee personal time seemed a bit of a miracle in itself Kate thought, as they entered the office, where she led them down a hallway to a small but well-appointed conference room. Her co-workers' heads turned only momentarily as they passed, before returning to their tasks at hand. White nodded but said nothing as the trio walked by his office.

Once the agents were seated, Kate treated them as she would have a client, first pouring coffee, then offering bottled water, before taking a chair herself.

Agent Rott had opened a portfolio and was sorting through papers as he looked up into her eyes, smiled and asked, "how much did you know about your husband's job when you married?"

"What do you mean?" Kate answered, having been taken off guard. "He told me he worked for the TSA and I just assumed that meant checking luggage at the airport and watching for illegals and those bent on doing harm to our government."

"So, you never met his superiors or had occasion to go to his place of work?" he continued, ignoring her question.

"I, we, know Tom Bridges and his wife. He was Tim's direct supervisor before we transferred out here to New Mexico. We were close friends with them and still are, but the need to see his office or meet with co-workers never came up," she explained. "Why? What does that have to do with Tim's disappearance?"

The agent looked at her hard before continuing in a gentler tone. "Homeland Security is a name which covers a lot of ground," he explained. "Tim's assignment was considerably more than just checking baggage."

"Who else knows about his disappearance?" agent Short asked, speaking now for the first time.

"My mother and father," she answered, "and I guess their prayer team at church, and now Mr. White I suppose."

Short frowned, then said, "we did not explain the reason for our discussion with your boss, but just that we just urgently needed to speak with you privately. Where do your parents live?"

"In Duluth. What difference does that make?" Kate asked in a rising tone. "I want to know what you are getting at, is Tim in trouble?"

"All the difference," Short answered, ignoring her question again. "But it is unlikely that anyone locally would have ties with a church group two thousand miles away."

Rott took over the conversation at this point. "There are things we can share with you and things we cannot for security reasons and for your personal safety, do you understand?"

Kate nodded, but did not answer.

Agent Rott seemed to be considering how and what to say before he spoke again. "Your husband has been working undercover with a joint task force for the past several months investigating smuggling of guns, drugs, and illegals who may be working to undermine our government. Were you aware of this?"

They could tell by her reaction that Kate had known nothing of her husband's double life.

"We can tell you that DNA tests proved the blood in the vehicle was his, but the small amount of blood would also indicate the injury was minor and not life threatening. We feel it is possible that it was left intentionally, possibly to throw someone off his trail," he explained.

Kate bit her lower lip before asking, "you think then, that they know he's working for the government and are trying to kill him? Why hasn't he contacted someone at Homeland Security to help him?"

"We don't know," Rott answered. "It is just possible there's a leak in the agency and he knows it and doesn't know who he can trust."

He can trust me," Kate answered, now beginning to cry softly.

"You are the last person he'd contact," agent Short answered. "He'd never purposely put you in danger."

"What do we do then?" she asked.

"With your permission, we think we should put information out on the media confirming his disappearance and suspected abduction to support his story if he's just hiding out," agent Rott replied. "They obviously do not know where he is or why he has disappeared any more than we do. We'll play up the blood aspect and make it sound like we believe he was killed before his car was abandoned."

"What do I do?" she asked.

"Just go along with it and play the part of the worried wife,"

Rott answered. "Our best bet is that he may contact Bridges and Bridges will let us know."

"Unless...." she began, before stopping.

"Unless Bridges is the leak," he said, finishing the sentence for her. "But that is the chance we'll have to take, I see no other option."

The news broke later than evening, announcing that a local man had been missing for several days and that authorities suspected foul play due to the condition of his abandoned vehicle. After a full analysis of the vehicle was complete, considerable animal blood had been poured onto the driver' seat before photos were released to the public. A very short bio mentioned his name, that he was new to the area, married, and that he had worked only a short time for Southwest Trucking Company, all of which was true. The release did not mention that the investigation was now in the hands of the FBI.

"Tom, Tom Bridges?" said an inquiring tone into the phone. "this is Special Agent John Rott with the FBI out in New Mexico, do you have a few minutes to visit?"

"Yes, this is Tom, what can I do for you, Agent Rott?" came the reply.

"I was told that Tim Roberts was a co-worker and friend of yours, is that accurate?" Rott asked, in a business-like manner.

"That is true, I was his supervisor until he transferred, and he and his wife are our friends," he continued. "Is something wrong?"

The agent knew he had to tell the truth if he expected help but did not want to tell any more than necessary if it turned out Bridges was involved.

"He has disappeared, his vehicle was found abandoned with a broken window, and with blood evidence inside. DNA confirms it is his blood and it is being considered a possible abduction or murder," the agent related.

There was a long pause as Bridges absorbed what he had heard. "Is Kate alright? Is she also missing?"

Rott noted that there seemed a lack of surprise at his announcement.

"No, she's obviously upset and worried, but she is physically fine. She gave us your name as a possible contact person that he might call if he is alive and is able to find a way to ask for help. Are you aware of the nature of his current assignment?" he asked candidly.

"I am not at liberty to discuss this matter further on an unsecure line," Bridges answered. "I'll speak to my director and return your call from my office after I confirm your identity."

"Agreed," Agent Rott said. "But please limit who you tell and keep it on a need-to-know basis."

It was 7:00 a.m. local time when the call was transferred to Rott's office phone, making it 9:00 a.m. on the east coast.

"Good morning Agent Rott," Tom said pleasantly. "Do you have any more news about Tim?"

"We do not," the agent replied. "Are you able to share any information which may aid in our investigation?"

Bridges went on to tell a story which seemed too incredible to believe. A story of a syndicate of co-conspirators from coast to coast, each with their own profit motive, who had joined forces and assets in the areas of drugs, human trafficking, prostitution, illegal guns and explosives, and anti-American subversives, who had been allowed across our borders with impunity by the past political regime.

"Their operation seems to be centered in or around

Albuquerque, New Mexico, which caused us to put our best men on the ground there, which included Tim Roberts," Tom said. "We have credible evidence that two of his counterparts have already been found dead, which may indicate a leak. I suppose that in an operation of this size, which involves several agencies and hundreds of operatives, that is not totally unexpected."

"So, you are viewing this in much the same way as we are here," Rott answered, "a possible inside job. He was apparently fired the day he disappeared, but we have yet to interview his employer about the details of his termination. My personal belief is that he knew his time was running out and staged his own disappearance, hoping with all the players involved that each may think the other took him out."

"If that is the case," he continued, "I would expect him to try and contact you personally."

The connection was silent for a short time before Tom Bridges answered. "We have a strict compartmentalization protocol that would preclude Tim reaching out to anyone but his own handler. Unfortunately, his direct up-line was one of the two found murdered last week."

"So..." Rott replied, "that leaves him adrift, alone, and without support, if I read you correctly.

"He's smart and capable," Tom answered. "I don't think anyone will find him until he's ready to be found. Do you have Kate in a secure location?"

"We have two men on her 24/7," agent Rott replied, "but I thought it best to let her maintain her schedule, hoping the enemy may think he's been killed by one of the other members of the syndicate."

"I've an idea, I'll share it with you when I get there," Bridges said. "My plane arrives in Albuquerque tonight at 6:00 p.m."

"I'll be wearing a red **MAGA** ball cap," Rott said, laughing. "See you then."

Bridges was a tall man, well over six feet, with sandy blond hair and smile wrinkles around his mouth that testified of a man who loved life. Rott estimated him to be in his early 40's as he approached, taking long confident strides.

"Mr. Bridges," the agent said while extending his right hand, "I'm John Rott, welcome to **The Land of Enchantment**."

They clasped hands and took a moment to size each other up before leaving the terminal with only Tom's carry-on.

"Hungry?" Rott asked, smiling. "I thought maybe we could talk over dinner."

Bridges returned his smile and answered, "starving!"

The southwest cuisine proved to be all that Tom had expected and more, which forced the two men to postpone conversation until the dessert arrived.

"I've brought some photos of Tim with me," Tom began. "Photos that were taken when the four of us were spending time together. My thought is that someone in your agency, with the right skills, could photoshop several of them to create a realistic crime scene collage that could be leaked to the press."

"Genius!" John exclaimed. "Why didn't I think of that?"

Tom didn't reply, but instead smiled before shoveling another big bite of mud pie into his mouth.

John took the bill from the waitress before Tom could argue and said, "my treat."

They visited like they had known each other all of their lives as John drove toward the Howard Johnson where Tom had reservations. John could easily see why Kate had expressed a special fondness for him and his wife. He hoped one day soon Tim would be joining them for a few beers, and they could share war stories.

"A favor?" Tom asked, before leaving the car to go inside, "Could you arrange a clandestine meeting with Kate so that we can talk. If anyone is watching her, I do not want to compromise our plan by announcing my arrival."

"You got it. I'll speak with her tonight and set it up for tomorrow morning," John answered. "Anything else?"

Tom handed him an envelope containing the photographs, opened the door, and said, "let your guys have a look and see what they can come up with."

The agency had a considerable archive of crime scene photos to choose from, some fit the body type, season, and location more than others. In the end, four sets were chosen and prepared for Tom's scrutiny and delivered by John the next morning.

"Kate has been registered as a guest in room 212 and will arrive this morning about ten o'clock by commercial taxi, driven by one of my agents," John explained. "She's been told only that someone wants to meet with her concerning Tim's disappearance."

"Thank you," Tom replied softly, as he viewed the photos with a pained expression on his face. "These are too good," he said, while swallowing a lump in his throat. "I hesitate to show these to Kate but I know I must."

~   ~

Cardoza was sitting across the table from Ben Sanders in his office at the truck terminal, drinking yet another glass of Jose Cuervo and looking at the morning paper. The front page showed several pictures of the body of a murder victim which had been found in the desert by a tourist. It had been identified by the police as Tim Roberts, a local truck driver who had been missing for over a week. The byline went on to recount details from earlier stories that described his abandoned vehicle and his mysterious disappearance.

"Well," he said in a heavy Spanish accent, pointing to the pictures with an evil grin, "I guess that takes care of all the loose ends."

Sanders nodded his agreement and joined his colleague in a splash of the warm, amber liquid. It had been he who had caught Tim snooping through his office after hours, and it was he who had followed him to a late-night meeting with the first two victims. He'd notified Cardoza and the others, who had ordered the hits.

Ben Sanders thought of himself as both a valuable and equal partner with Cardoza and the others, which of course he was not. He was just a greedy trucking company owner who had no conscience and an inflated ego. In reality, the syndicate had already considered eliminating him and finding another like himself, who could be more easily controlled.

~ ~

Tim pondered as he lay under the cheap blue tarp, surrounded by the homeless and hopeless of the city, what his next move should be. With the deaths of Jakes and Bishop, his contact with Homeland Security had effectively been severed. Who or how their cover had been blown, he was at a loss to know and until he knew, he was taking no chances! He spoke fluent Spanish and had purposely let his black hair grow long and ragged over the past several weeks, his skin color had been darkened with the use of brown shoe polish, making it easy for him to acclimate with both the legal and illegal refugees who lived with him on the streets.

The picture in the 2-day old newspaper that lined the inside of his worn-out shoe didn't seem to resemble him in the least. However, as he had looked at it and read the account of his murder, he could almost believe it himself. His life, his real life, seemed now almost a fairytale. His mind turned to Kate and wondered as he drifted into a restless sleep, what pain he had caused her and if he survived, could they ever again be the young, carefree couple they once were.

Tom and his wife stood beside Kate and her parents across the graveside from John Rott and the other mourners, as the pastor quoted from memory Bible verses that he hoped would give some peace and hope to those who had known and loved Tim Roberts.

A hundred yards away, a black limousine with four men inside was parked; they were carefully watching the ceremony through binoculars. Unnoticed by anyone, a wino sat with his back against the cemetery fence to the far left, drinking from a bottle wrapped in a wrinkled brown paper bag. The irony of the situation nearly caused Tim to laugh as he pretended to take another swig from the long-necked bottle in his hand. However, the pain he knew that his family and friends were enduring stifled his momentary levity.

He wondered how and when he'd find a way to contact Tom and if that was prudent, given the circumstances. The limo did not go unnoticed by Tim or other FBI agents pretending to be mourners. Several blocks away, still other agents took dozens of photos with long range lenses, both of the limo and of the small group gathered at the graveside. At the family's request, there had been no church service or open casket viewing. Cardoza, his driver, Sanders, and a body guard remained until the mourners began to leave for their cars.

"What do you think?" Tom asked John. "Do you think they have any reason to believe the funeral was bogus?"

"It felt real to me," John answered. "My heart was breaking

for all those who came and were not privy to the information. It's such a shame we couldn't at least tell Kate's mother and father."

"Now we wait," Tom answered his new friend's unasked question, as they left the cemetery.

~   ~

Tim went into the little store on the corner and bought a bottle of MD 20/20. He didn't have to ask the clerk to put it in a brown bag. Then he went to the front desk at the Howard Johnson and before they could usher him out, paid the desk clerk $20 to send it to room 213 with his compliments. When Tom opened the door and received the gift from the bellman, he immediately understood its meaning.

"He's gone underground, living on the streets," he said in an excited voice, "Hiding in plain sight. We need to go shopping."

John stood, with a puzzled look on his face.

They left the room separately, and discreetly exited from the rear facing entrance where a car was waiting for them. A few minutes later, they entered the Salvation Army store and began to shop. Undressing and redressing in the rear seat of the car, they emerged looking every bit like street people, save for freshly washed faces and shaved cheeks.

"It'll have to do," Tom said, as he looked in the side mirror and grinned at John. "We don't have time to mess with makeup or a fake beard."

Evening was fast upon them, with street lights coming on automatically, as the sun dropped behind the surrounding mountains. John noticed that Tom had adopted a shuffling gait and a semi-crouch, which hid his tall, athletic figure. He smiled to himself as pictures of The Walking Dead came to mind. They walked unsteadily beside one another, each with a bottle of cheap wine clutched in their hand, ambling along, apparently with no particular destination in mind.

Each dipped their fingers into the dirty grease on the hinge of a dumpster before applying it to their faces. As the streets became narrow and traffic less frequent, more and more shadowy faceless people like themselves appeared from the gloom. Makeshift shelters of cardboard or packing crates lined the ever narrowing streets. Here and there, small fires burned, billowing acrid smoke from abandoned metal buckets or rusting barrels.

"We'll never find him this mess," John Rott whispered. "I can barely see my hand in front of my face."

"We won't have to," Tom answered. "He'll find us."

~   ~

"Tim is fine," Kate confided to her parents.

But before she could explain, her mother spoke. "I know, by the blood of Jesus we'll all see him again."

"He's alive," Kate said. "I couldn't tell anyone because he's in hiding and has killers looking for him. I'm sorry to have let you go through this but there was no other way to keep him safe unless they truly believe he is dead."

She went on to tell them what Tom and John had shared with her making, them first promise not to share the good news with anyone, including their church friends at home.

"They are out looking for him now," she explained, "with the goal to find him and take him somewhere where he'll be safe. I do not understand it all myself, but he was apparently working undercover for the government."

They visited long into the night before finally succumbing to the rigors of the day and giving in to exhaustion.

~   ~

"You have any cigarettes?" a beggar asked, as they passed by his hooch.

"Sorry, don't smoke," Tom answered automatically, before continuing on.

The man caught Tom by the arm, looked at him curiously and said, "I didn't ask you if you smoked, I asked if you have any cigarettes."

John was surprised to see Tom smiling before he heard, "Tim? Is that you?"

A minute later, the three had disappeared into the darkness and were sitting under the makeshift shelter, leaning back against an aging chain link fence. They spoke in muted tones, as nearly everyone in the community also seemed to do.

"Sanders caught me in his office after hours," Tim explained. "I had no excuse and no reason to be there so he fired me on the spot. But not before I found information about the location and date of a high-level meeting of the six cartels, which I passed on to Jakes and Bishop. He must have followed me to our meet."

"So," Tom said smiling to himself in the darkness, "it appears maybe we don't have a leak after all. Are you ready to come in?"

"More than ready," his friend answered. "I haven't had a shower in three weeks."

"We noticed!" John and Tom laughed simultaneously.

The three stood, set their wine bottles on the ground in the enclosure, and walked briskly to where their waiting vehicle was parked. A short time later, they re-parked behind the Howard Johnson, took the stairs to the second floor and entered room 212.

"You get cleaned up," Bridges ordered. "I have some calls to make."

The bedside clock read 2:17 a.m. when Kate groggily reached

for her cell phone, after the fourth ring.

"Allo," she answered bruskly. "Do you know what time it is?"

"Sure do," Tom answered jovially, "time for breakfast. I've called room service and ordered us a big celebration breakfast. I'll have taxi waiting out front for you in ten minutes."

When she entered, she was filled with anticipation and happiness, which was only magnified at the sight of Tim standing smiling across the room. A dozen men from both agencies were already partaking from the tables filled with food, and as she ran to her husband, they began to clap their hands. An hour later, the couple left, crossed the hallway, and disappeared into their own world, only to reappear about noon the next day, still smiling happily.

"The official news of Tim's miraculous resurrection in the local paper was not in print until a week later, after the NSA, FBI, CIA, DEA, Homeland Security, and Justice Department dropped the hammer and arrested nearly 300 in the initial raid, Cardoza and Sanders among them. For a short time following the arrests and prosecution of the cartels, Kate and Tim basked in the glow of being reunited and feeling blessed to have been fortunate to have dodged the bullet.

However, like many things, as the glow faded, Kate began to feel resentment, disillusionment, and even anger that the man she had married had purposefully withheld information, which had affected them so greatly. She became quiet and withdrawn, rebuffing his attempts to cheer her or find out the cause of her moodiness. Like most men, he considered the event as being behind them and was eager to move forward. Like many women, she felt betrayed and wounded and clung fiercely to her pain, justifying and growing it by doing so.

One night, following still another rebuff trying to initiate intimacy, Tim became angry, raised his voice and demanded to know what her problem was. In tears born of hurt and anger, she replied in kind, and they had their first fight. Tim spent his first night in the guest room. The next morning, he found her in the kitchen at the table sipping coffee. He joined her.

"I'm going to visit my parents for a while," she declared tonelessly. He started to respond but thought better of it and nodded.

"Honey, I'm sorry," he finally said. "I shouldn't have raised my voice."

Kate looked at him coldly and answered. "You still don't get it, do you? You lied to me, our whole marriage has been a lie, and I look at you and don't know who I'm seeing. The man I married, or someone on a secret mission, acting a part."

"But, but..." he began, in an effort to explain his side of the story.

"Don't you but, but me," she replied, with fire in her eyes. "I've spent over a week in prayer with my parents, pouring over the Bible for comfort, wondering if you were alive or dead, and now you come home and try to explain it all away. Look at it from my perspective, the "*job*" is the other woman and you are with her, secretly planning things together, which we do not share."

"I... I'm sorry," he began again, trying to express what he was now feeling.

Kate was holding her well-worn Bible in her hands, with tears continuing to run down her cheeks, as she opened it to Matthew 6:24 and began to read: "Man cannot serve two masters, for either he will hate the one and love the other or he will hold to the one and despise the other. He cannot serve God and riches."

Her voice dropped and became emotional, as tears continued to flow. "You will have to choose between us and your secret life that excludes me and is destroying us."

She stood and left the room, which left Tim to reflect upon their spiritual, physical, and emotional commitments to each other. In the beginning, they had attended church regularly and shared a desire to follow and know Jesus better. Gradually their attendance and commitment to Him became less and less, as they let the demands of everyday life interfere with that commitment. Paradoxically, Tim's desire to move closer to Jesus seemed to always be countered by something in life seemingly more urgent or demanding.

The next morning, Tim had just stepped out of the shower and stood towel wrapped, wiping the steam off of the mirror, while he groomed for his first day back at work since the trials had ended. Kate had already showered and left the bathroom for the kitchen, where she was perusing the newspaper and drinking a cup of coffee. As he worked to comb his shaggy hair, he made a note to see the barber before returning home that night. The haze of the steam seemed to be difficult to wipe away and the more he tried, the clearer the images in the mirror became.

Three faces returned his gaze, the first was the man he currently was, the one just returning from undercover, who looked tired, worn, and beleaguered. The second stood to the left and was a replica of the man he had been when they had married; young, vital, with an eagerness to embrace life. The one in the center did not seem to represent him at all, at least not as he would have pictured himself. Its features were indistinct and less severe, they held no sign of stress or worry, and its smile seemed engaging and drew him toward it. A singular thought floated through his mind, "that is who I'd like to be." Only to be answered immediately by a thought which said, "that is who you are."

The ambient temperature in the kitchen was far better than

it had been the evening before in the bedroom, but even so he could feel tension, as he joined his wife at the table with a steaming mug of coffee. "Need a warm-up?" Tim asked pleasantly, referring to her coffee.

Kate smiled and handed him her cup, but did not answer when he refilled it and handed it back to her.

"I'd like to show you something," Tim began, "if you'll come to the bathroom with me."

Kate followed behind him until they stood side-by-side, facing his mirror.

"What do you see?" he asked.

"I see us," she answered, in an irritated tone.

"Step to one side and tell me what you see," he urged.

Kate moved to where the only reflection visible to her was her husband.

"I see you," she answered tiredly, while wondering what sort of a game Tim was playing.

"Oh!" she exclaimed, placing a hand over her mouth. "What, who is that?"

Tim was smiling broadly when he said, "that's what I just asked myself."

Kate now moved beside him, but saw no image of herself reflected, only the three faces in the mirror remained. She squeezed his arm, and smiled up at him then said, "that's easy... the one on the left is you as you are today, the one on the right is the one who you were when we married, and one in the center is the one God sees when He looks at you."

A lump in his throat and tears in his eyes evidenced that he realized what she had said was true; he knew now why he'd been drawn to the third figure, the one smiling back at him. The one that represented the heart of Jesus.

In closing, let me just say that Tim's request for job reassignment was granted, and his commitment to Jesus and Kate was restored. They are currently expecting their first child, a ***child of promise***.

The Sacrifice

I remember my life seemed so happy and blessed. I had a beautiful wife and two children, all of who were healthy and happy as well. With the many years I spent in college behind me, they were just beginning to bear fruit as my dental practice began to grow and provide a reliable source of income for us. The word "blessed", as used often in Christian speech summed it up well, God had chosen to "bless us." I remember distinctly the day that all changed.

~   ~

"Good morning, doctor," my receptionist Sheila said, as she always did, when I arrived at the office. "A man left this for you," she added, while holding a plain white envelope out toward me.

"A patient?" I asked over my shoulder, as I continued toward my office without opening it.

"I didn't recognize him," she replied.

I tossed the envelope on my desk and poured myself a cup of coffee and donned my white lab coat before sitting down and slipping my fingers under the seal. Inside was a sheet of white bond paper, with a single sentence printed across it.

It read, ***I've finally found you and now you will pay for the pain you have caused me***. It must be a mistake, I thought immediately, while trying to remember when or to whom I could have done something to warrant such a threat.

Two weeks went by and I had almost forgotten the letter until a second one arrived at my office by mail. It said, *I thought about killing your family like you did mine, but have decided to give you an opportunity to save them*.

My heart nearly stopped as I read and reread the note and its reference to my family. The memory of a singular event years before pushed its way into my mind, the memory of a day I tried, but could never quite forget. As a senior in college, I had attended a frat party where of course there was loud music, free flowing alcohol, and willing young women. On my way home, I had passed out behind the wheel of my car and crossed over the centerline into oncoming traffic. I had spent seven of my 15-year sentence in prison before being released on parole to begin a new life. I had finished college, married, gotten my dental license, and had two children since.

My mood must have shown on my face as my wife asked with concern, "didn't you sleep well last night?" I remember mumbling something but did not share my concerns with her since she had no knowledge of my dark past.

Another two weeks passed before I received yet another threatening communication which said, *the time has come, read John 15:13 and make your choice*.

I hurriedly retrieved my worn Bible and found the described verse which said, *"Greater love has no man than this, that a man lay down his life for his friends."*

The verse and its meaning were familiar to me, Christ knew He must die that others may live, and in much the same manner I had to be willing to face death if necessary, so that my family would live. The considerable difference of course was that Jesus was blameless and I was guilty as charged.

Time passed slowly and with it, an ever-increasing sense of fear and dread. My family and employees began to openly question my health and state of mind, as I arrived at work disheveled and preoccupied. Monday, two weeks to the day later, the morning mail held a final communication which I feverishly opened, it read, ***Meet me Friday at 6:00 p.m. at 1604 Maple Street. Come alone and be prepared to receive your judgment***.

I parked my car at the end of the street and walked down Maple Street, past decaying structures built after the Second World War. Little cookie cutter boxes, cheaply made to accommodate the returning GI's, lined both sides of the street. Most appeared vacant, only a few of them were lighted or showed any sign of habitation. The few street lights still operational flickered intermittently, as though they wanted to join their darkened peers.

I walked on wooden legs toward the old house as my heart filled with dread. The ***For Sale by Owner*** sign in the front yard was nearly hidden by weeds and overgrown shrubbery, but the house numbers still showed plainly on the weathered siding, beside the front door. This is ***it*** I said to myself as fear nearly choked me, ***my time has come***.

As I approached the house, I could see a single light burning in the kitchen area, the rest of the house was as dark as the devil's heart. I looked at my watch, it read 5:58 p.m., before I gingerly knocked on the weathered wooden door. As the door opened into the room, a stooped figure was back-lit by a single naked bulb hanging from the ceiling, over an ancient kitchen table.

"Come in," he said, almost pleasantly. "I've been expecting you."

I swallowed hard before replying, "I'm Benjamin Nelson."

"Of course you are," he replied cordially. "Please have a seat at the table."

"Tea?" he asked, as he hefted a large pot full of boiling water and poured the steaming liquid into two small cups, with tea bags already in them.

As he sat the pot back on the stove, I remember thinking how odd it seemed, to be threatened with retribution and at the same time being offered a cup of tea, as though we were old friends.

He seated himself across from me and began toying with the tea bag while waiting for it to steep. Finally, he raised his eyes to mine and asked, "*have you made your decision?*"

I dropped my eyes from his penetrating stare, hesitated, and then answered "I am so sorry for the pain I've caused you…"

He interrupted. "You haven't any idea of my pain," he said harshly. "You're far past due and any apology given under duress is worthless." He stopped speaking and sipped his tea, while looking curiously at me across the table.

"*An eye for and eye*," he said quoting again from scripture, "*and a tooth for a tooth*. Isn't that what the Good Book says?"

I caught his meaning all too well, but chose not to answer, knowing he was referring to both his family and my own.

"I've had years to think about the meaning of this and to pray that God would guide me to the correct decision regarding how to deliver judgment," he said, almost sadly. "Never a day has passed since you took them from me, that I haven't felt pain and I am forever scarred by my loss."

I sat waiting, thinking that under other circumstances, this man and I could have been friends, and knowing that whatever came I had to accept it for myself, my family, and for his peace.

He stood, moved toward the stove where he retrieved the boiling pot of water, before turning back toward the table and refilling the two tea cups. As I reached out my hands toward the cup, he poured the remaining water across both of my hands and arms. The last thing I remembered before waking up, was my own scream and the intolerable pain as the boiling liquid melted the flesh from my body.

When I awakened, he was gone, both of my arms had been carefully bound in sterile gauze from the elbows down and lay throbbing on the table in front of me. My cell phone lay face up facing me, showing that 911 had been dialed. Outside, I could hear the sound of sirens searching for their destination.

As a result of my disfigured hands, I've lost my practice and with it, my home and comfortable lifestyle. Never a day passes now that I don't feel pain, and it is seldom that someone does not notice my many scars, avert their eyes, or remark about them.

Of Men and Women

What little we men know about the opposite sex we have mostly learned from our mistakes, and those of others like ourselves. God's plan, be it perfect or not, seems from my humble perspective, somewhat flawed. We may as well from birth be from different worlds, cultures, or races for what little we have in common is far less than what one would suppose. That we are anatomically different should be evident but why we cannot communicate what we see and feel remains to me a mystery.

~   ~

"Where shall we eat," I asked, expecting that she'd have a preference of restaurants, or at least cuisine.

"I don't care, wherever you like," she answered disinterestedly.

Encouraged, I suggested, "how about **KFC**, we haven't been there in a while."

"No, not **KFC**. Anywhere else, but not there," she said.

Disappointed but not surprised, I tried again, "How about **Chinese** then, Chinese sounds good to me."

She made a face, which told me **strike two**, before she answered, "Okay, if that's what you want, but I had noodles for lunch yesterday."

Trying to avoid a confrontation and ruin our night out, I offered, "you choose then. Anywhere you want is fine with me."

She didn't take the bait, instead she repeated her previous, "I don't care, you decide."

By now, I sensed an almost imperceptible coolness had entered our conversation and I realized I should choose my words carefully, or lose everything I'd hope to accomplish when I suggested our dinner out.

I started to say **Golden Corral**, because of the diversity of their menu but thought better of it. "**Olive Garden**?" I asked, with a question in my voice, as though thinking out loud.

"That's **fine**," she said, but by the tone I could tell it wasn't fine at all, maybe just barely acceptable and that further conversation was risky.

I turned the car toward our new location without a word, parked, and tried to seem excited about enjoying the meal as we walked in together silently, and were seated.

~   ~

I am by nature a planner, an organizer, and I'd like to think dependable and logical because of it. I'd rather be early to a promised event by an hour, than late by ten minutes. I'm not asking you to judge me, just understand me. So then when she rebuffed my suggestion for the coming Friday night, I was taken off-guard.

"We can't. We are going to the Jones' Friday night for dinner. Did you forget?" she said accusingly.

"When did we decide that?" I asked, wondering if I'd forgotten the discussion.

"You were there," she answered smugly. "We talked about it after church Sunday."

"I don't remember us deciding anything Sunday, what I do remember is you women visiting, and we men were visiting, but nothing was brought up about dinner," I said, a bit too defensively.

"You were right there when **we** decided," she said firmly.

We, of course, meant the women.

Dead meat, I thought to myself, having walked this pathway before about my choice not to eavesdrop their conversation and therefore not hear their decision.

"What time?" I asked, trying to move forward.

"About 6:00," she answered, "we're bringing a salad and a dessert."

Now I knew I had not been involved in the conversation at all because I'd certainly have remembered at least the time or menu.

As a man, it makes me wonder if they **listen in** on men's conversations the way they seem to think we do to them. I will never know because I will never ask.

~   ~

Dangerously close to the edge describes it well, not unlike traveling on a single-track mountain road with a sheer drop off on one side. There are a few oddities that have become jokes and are more or less safe to talk about. Many show up on Facebook or in cartoons. For example:

The woman sporting her new jeans asks her husband innocently, "do these make me look fat?"

Or...

"You didn't say anything about my hair. Don't you like it?"

Or...

"How do you like my new recipe?"

Or simply...

"What do you think?"

Maybe I should have titled this **Trip-ups & Traps for Men**. If this seems one-sided to you, note that I cannot write the other side of this comparison, because I haven't a clue about the workings of the female mind.

Okay men, has anyone noticed as the male in the family mellows with age, the female adopts a need to take charge and treat him like he was not in the room, or that his opinion is of little value? Don't answer honestly or you are sleeping in the garage.

A Vision of Creation

Often, it seems, intellect and reason impede our growth in faith. We use reason and our life experiences to try to explain the unexplainable, thus leaving us to question that faith. Recently, I was given information without seeking it, while trying to get to sleep. Much of it is far above my education and intelligence level, causing me to consider if it was not from the Holy Spirit and thus, I am sharing it with you.

~   ~

Mankind has long wondered from where he came, and to where he will go when he dies. The Bible tells us in general terms, relying upon our faith to make those answers acceptable, without getting into details. We, however, seem to always want the details.

Consider the possibility that our souls – our spirits – are simply intelligent energy created by God, not unlike the light which is transmitted via fiberoptic cable. In the infinite universe, there is but one which God has chosen to harbor life, our planet earth. Unseen to us, the third planet from our sun is surrounded by billions of "energy spirits," waiting to be sent to the proper place at the proper time by God.

Try and picture the sphere surrounded by beams of light energy steadily coming and going to and from earth, as one of God's children is conceived, while another breathes their last breath. Heaven is the name we have given to this holding place, where both they and God dwell. It is also the place where the "saved" in Jesus go while waiting for the end of times, when He will come back and there will be a New Heaven and a New Earth.

Unconventional yes, impossible no; nothing is impossible to God. If you think this explanation is too simple, consider first our salvation is seemingly too simple to many religious folks and yet the Bible describes it so. It is not by works, good deeds, or our best efforts, but by declaring Jesus as our Lord and Savior, that we find eternal life, because of His willingness to die in our place.

When Our Best is Not Good Enough

Have you ever been in the unenviable position where you are doing what you feel is your best and it doesn't satisfy someone else? Nearly everyone has, and most have then been forced to handle the situation without knowing the best method to address it. Be it a job, a marriage, or a friendship, few people share the same sense of duty or responsibility to a relationship.

First, look inward and try to impartially evaluate both your skill level and your commitment, then try and determine if your performance falls short or if the expectation is more than you can fulfill. This is difficult, in that we are truly not the best judge of our own abilities. This is almost certainly why God is our Judge and why Jesus had to die to atone for our sins.

Works-based religions operate under the false premise that ***our good enough is good enough***, without having any concept of what true perfection requires. True perfection does not exist in man – any man – only in God.

~   ~

Contrary to the way some describe the sound of the ball

passing through the net without touching the rim, there is no "swish," or at least not one audible enough to be heard by the fans. Ted had just scored another trey, his third, and it was only five minutes into the first quarter. The score was 12-6, with the Mustangs leading their cross-town rivals. The Cougars brought the ball down court in their usual manner, while attempting to get a handle on the new offense the Mustangs had adopted this season. In past years, the two teams had been evenly matched, and nearly always met in the state finals in a hard-fought game to win bragging rights for that year.

Ted is a senior, a point guard, and Captain of the team. His natural leadership qualities, both off and on the court and history as a four-year varsity man, had several universities looking seriously at him. Tall, handsome in a rough sort of way, and naturally charismatic, he'd been a shoe-in for class president. It seemed to most that he had it all, and that his life was on auto-pilot, promising great things in the future.

Decker, the Cougar's guard, tested Ted, before passing cross court to the off guard, and then to the forward, who tried a three which bounced off the rim and was taken down by Vince, the Mustang center. Opportunity missed, Ted thought, as he expertly dribbled down court, before sending the ball zinging toward the backboard, where Vince grabbed the Alley-Oop and dunked it effortlessly. Vince was 6'-6" and Ted's best friend; they had played ball of one sort or another since grade school, sharing their lives without reservation.

Vince had the skill but not the bulk or desire to move up to the next level where tall, gifted athletes like himself out-weighed him by nearly a hundred pounds. Ted suspected that he was only playing now because he knew his friend and his teammates needed him. He was quiet and introspective, nearly shy, where Ted was outgoing and extroverted. They complimented each other well, both on and off the court.

By the half, the Mustangs had a commanding lead, the score stood at 49-24, which unfortunately made them become complacent. The Cougars dropped in a trey and picked up a foul on the play to cut the lead and gain momentum. Decker stole the ball from Ted, ran the court, and jammed it in for two more. The Mustangs were on their heels, reeling from the run and without a plan, when their Coach called time-out. He was looking right at Ted when he said, "get your head in the game or lose it, it's as simple as that. They want to win more than you do."

Forty-nine to thirty still seemed an insurmountable lead as they began to trade points going into the third quarter. Suddenly Decker got hot, dropping in treys back to back as his teammates began feeding him the ball. Ted aired out a three-pointer which was taken down by the Cougar's big man, before being lofted down court to Decker at a full run. In less than a minute, he'd cut the lead to 4. The scoreboard read 65-61 with five minutes left to play when Ted brought the ball down court. When he feigned a pass to his forward, Decker attempted to steal, but Ted took a step back and lofted the ball for the three, but missed. Vince got the rebound and banked it in for two. The crowd was on their feet when the Cougars called time out.

Returning to the court, the Mustangs led by 2 with 1:42 on the clock and Cougars in possession. Decker smiled at his nemesis and passed the ball around the horn, taking seconds off the clock, before dropping in a trey and drawing a foul in the process. The Mustangs were down 3 now, with :47 remaining, as Ted looked desperately for an open man. He found none. With 6 seconds left, he bounced a three off the rim and Vince put it in for two. The Cougars won by a point, as the disappointed Mustang fans left the gym, shaking their heads.

Vince went off to college on an academic scholarship, Ted to a university where he studied engineering. They stayed in touch and hung on spring and Christmas breaks, but never regained the sense of closeness they'd once felt. Decker was drafted into the NBA by Detroit in the 5th round and spent six seasons with them, before receiving a career-ending knee injury.

So, life goes on in the small town. Ted is now the owner of a small mechanical engineering firm, Vince, who is married with two children, is the pastor of the local church, and Decker became the high school basketball coach and history teacher.

Christmas at Home

Have you ever, as a child or perhaps even as an adult, walked by a home in the darkness and looked into the windows and imagined what it would have been like to be a part of that family? Possibly you knew the occupants well, or more likely you knew them only in passing from the name on the mail box. The old man, for example, and his dog who lived at the end of the lane that you often observed coming and going in his ancient pickup, had he ever been married, did they have children, had he ever been young and curious as you now were? Was his life ever anything more than sitting at the kitchen table reading, with a single yellow light illuminating the room?

And the family across the street with the nicely kept home that always had a beautiful Christmas tree, what would have it been like to grow up as one of their children? Was their home, as it seemed, always bustling with energy and non-stop activity, or was it really as mundane and lackluster as those others on the street?

~   ~

I remember it well, it was Christmas week, and Christmas day that year was on a Saturday. The festive mood had begun the weekend before, and when Kelly Ann drove into the driveway late on

Wednesday night, snow was falling hard and had been since mid-afternoon. Several inches were now covering the streets and side-walks and hiding the starkness of the barren trees in our front yard. We'd worried that the first big snowfall of the year might make traveling difficult or dangerous for our little brood and had cautioned each of them to drive carefully and keep us apprised of their progress.

Kelly, who lived on the other side of town, was our middle daughter, the one who should have learned from the mistakes of her older siblings but had not. She'd been married twice, the first time right out of high school and was now, as far as we knew, single again. As parents do, we worried that her three children would never have an intact home or a father-figure to give them the stability which she always seemed to lack.

All the same, we were overjoyed to see them arrive safely, full of smiles and with arms full of presents to arrange under the tree. We were not, however, overjoyed when her latest boyfriend and roommate followed her into the house. He had the appearance of a poster boy for the local homeless shelter and hardly seemed to have enough energy to speak when she introduced him simply as Ben.

Kelly Ann, or KA (pronounced Kay) as the family called her, had turned 26 in October and held a job as a nurse at a nearby hospital. Her nurse's salary allowed her to get by, but little more, since neither of her deadbeat ex-husbands helped them out financially. From all appearances she had found another, much like the previous two. Meg and I had given up trying to talk to her and only offered financial help when it seemed our grandchildren were suffering from her poor choices. We pray a lot and trust in God's plan for her life.

"Anyone hungry?" Meg asked the group after they taken off their coats and found seats in our living room.

Our grandchildren squealed, jumped to their feet and followed her into the kitchen, where a large pot of homemade chicken noodle soup was simmering. It seemed the mere mention of food gave Ben a needed energy boost because he beat the kids to the table and sat waiting, as Megan dished up the food and set out freshly made bread. KA looked a little put-off when he jumped in and began to eat before I had a chance to ask God's blessing on the food, but said nothing.

Meg and I listened patiently as the children talked in between bites. I remember making a mental head count which was now seven, and wondering if the 25 lb. turkey waiting in the freezer would be enough for our large family. What to do with Ben, I asked myself. Regardless of what happens in her home, we don't allow non-marrieds to cohabit in ours. I made a mental note to speak with my wife about sleeping arrangements.

"Can we open just one?" Casey asked, as she crawled into my lap. "Pleeeze?"

I hesitated, as two other eager faces also turned their attention to me, then shook my head slowly before answering, "nope, we have to wait for others and then all of us can open one together on Christmas Eve."

I noted that Ben was eagerly holding out his bowl when Megan asked if anyone was ready for seconds. A few minutes later, when the feeding frenzy had abated, she served freshly baked sugar cookies, brightly decorated in the colors of the season, and hot chocolate. I smiled and settled back in my lounge chair to watch as our old dog made short work of the many crumbs which had fallen to the floor. I had been blessed, I thought, with a good career in the air force, before taking a job locally as an air traffic controller.

We still lived in our original house which had been added onto several times as our family had grown, thus allowing us to live comfortably now within our means. That I still was working was by choice, and not out of necessity.

"KA, you'll take Neecie's room," Meg announced, while leaving no room for discussion. "The kids can sleep in sleeping bags in front of the fireplace, and Ben... Tom will help you make up the hide-a-bed. Boo can sleep with us, if that's alright."

I could have kissed Meg right then but waited for a later time. She always had a way of getting things done without a long, drawn out argument. Neecie is our youngest daughter Denise, who is in her first year at college and her bed is a super single, which does not allow room for more than one.

Tom-Tom moved up next to me as I stood, and hugged my leg. He gave me a snaggle-toothed smile that melted my heart when he said, "I wove you Grammppy."

We ended up with all three grandchildren in our king-sized bed that first night.

Thursday morning found us blanketed in nearly a foot of fresh white, powdery snow. The children, of course, were anxious to get outside and play in it. A call from Alison, our oldest daughter, announced that their plane had been delayed but was scheduled to land before noon, and that she was bringing three with her that had nowhere to go for Christmas. Ali was 27 and had just re-upped in the Marines for the second time.

College had never been an option for her. She joined a month after graduating from high school, with the intention to make it a career. Interesting that she had accepted an offer to go to the academy, had graduated, and now wore the rank of second lieutenant.

We were warming by the fireplace, trying to dry out, when the doorbell rang. Megan answered it. Ali stood smiling, with three young men behind her, as two squealing children ran toward her screaming, "Aunt Ali." Tom-Tom of course had no idea who his aunt was, but followed his older sister's lead.

Respectful and disciplined would aptly describe the three tall, well-muscled young men whom she introduced first by their last names, as is the military way, before smiling and introducing them again by their first names. Ben, who had now stood, looked almost effeminate as he shook their hands and introduced himself. I wondered if KA possibly also had made the same observation.

Each man carried a ruck sack over his shoulder and a sleeping bag in his free hand. My head count was now eleven, I made that a dozen when Neecie suddenly opened the door and let herself in, just as I showed the Marines downstairs to our family room, where several foam mats were already placed on the shag carpet. I decided that Ben should also gravitate down and be with the other single men now that Neecie and Ali was also home. The hide-a-bed, which was a double, was more suitable for two of our girls than him.

Derek, Mary, and their family arrived Friday morning after driving all the way from Deerpoint on their way here from Denver. Thankfully, they'd stopped by the assisted living center and picked up Grace, which saved me going out into the snow. Grace, Megan's mother, was no longer able to live alone and although she still drove occasionally, she would now wisely leave her Oldsmobile parked until spring. Derek and Mary have two children, Billy, age eight, and Kate, age seven, and are expecting a third sometime in March. I know what you're thinking, but no, we're not Mormons or Catholics, we're just a family blessed by God to procreate and spread the "Good News."

The head count now was, I think, eighteen, but I rounded it to twenty, knowing that the Petersons, an older couple next door were always invited to enjoy Christmas dinner with us. They had no children and no living relatives in state which were fit to travel. Now as I remembered them, I reminded myself that I needed to take time to shovel their sidewalk and driveway, and made mental note to do so after everyone was settled in.

Our home was full of smiling, hungry, happy people when I took the TV trays and folding chairs from the closet, to supplement our large dining table. I was pleased to find several pairs of hands eager to help me arrange them. Derek smiled sheepishly as he and the three Marines stomped the snow off their feet and came inside from shoveling snow, just in time to sit down with the rest of the crew for breakfast. As I blessed the food and thanked the Lord for bringing our family together, I snuck a peek at Ben, who was waiting patiently head bowed, for the signal to eat.

Our daughters banished Megan from her kitchen as they began to clean up the breakfast dishes. She wrapped her hands around my arm and smiled sweetly up at me, and gave my arm a little squeeze, but said nothing.

"The Petersons are coming?" I asked, knowing they always had.

"Yes," she answered softly. "A couple of you should go a little early and walk them over."

Dinner on Friday night had a volume of food which Megan had prepared in advance and stored to be reheated later. We enjoyed spaghetti with meat balls, lasagna, green salad, and toasted French bread with garlic butter. With eighteen of our twenty at various tables, there was nothing wasted and nothing needing to be saved for later. Ice cream, fresh frozen California berries and whipped cream finished off the meal.

As the women filled the dishwasher, the children, both old and young, waited anxiously by the tree in anticipation of opening a gift. This not being my first rodeo, I had searched out and quickly wrapped several extra pair of new socks and t-shirts of my own, for our four surprise guests. Meg had, with Ali's help and without anyone taking notice, labeled each of them appropriately. Although nearly 80, Grace's eyes mirrored the twinkle that was apparent in our grandchildren. I marveled to myself at God's plan.

Derek, having grown up in a house full of women had adopted, possibly out of necessity, a great sense of humor. This year, when I had asked, he replaced me and had accepted the mantle of "gift giver". He passed out the presents with great solemnity, but always with a quip and appropriate comment. I remember thinking that our home was filled with love and how grateful I was.

That the various "*Santas*" had each done their respective duties and had slipped quietly out and deposited gifts under the tree without running into each other, was in itself a Christmas miracle. When shrieks of joy from the children awakened us on Christmas morning, we joined them around the tree, sipping hot coffee and waiting for the ceremony to kick off. Once again, Derek took center stage, where he began passing out the unwrapped "*Santa*" gifts first. The crowning moment was toward the end of the festivities when Clayton, one of the Marines, rose from his place on the floor, walked to the tree, and removed a small, beautifully wrapped gift which he them gave to Ali. It was an engagement ring!

Later, I watched as Megan slipped away to the kitchen and heated her oven for the big sausage and hash brown breakfast casseroles. She had made three and I wondered if they would be sufficient. They were, but like last night's dinner, barely so. It seems that it takes a lot of energy to open presents, laugh, smile, and revel in the moment.

After breakfast, discarded wrapping paper and un-needed

boxes filled our two big trash receptacles to the top, leaving the tree looking a little forlorn, even with its sparkling decorations and lights. There was a bustle of activity as the list of side dishes were confirmed and readied, and the turkey was stuffed and put into the oven to bake. We men adjourned and found our way to the garage, where we each received a snow shovel or broom. We began to clear our sidewalk and driveway, then headed over to the Petersons to do the same. I was grateful for the five young men who went to work eagerly, without any urging.

"Are we going to the pond?" Derek asked, as we finished and put our tools away.

"I smiled and answered, "I see no way around it after the way the children took to it last year."

It took nearly an hour to match the available ice skates with waiting feet, but finally we loaded up three vehicles and headed out with blankets, thermoses of hot chocolate, Christmas cookies, and coffee. Others before us had moved most of the snow to the side, which allowed skaters like ourselves to enjoy nearly a half-acre if ice.

This was the third year of our family's latest tradition, to go to the park pond and skate, after opening our presents, while dinner cooked. I was overjoyed to see that our children had brought with them skates for our grandchildren. I imagined that as the children grew, new skates for larger feet would be purchased and others would be passed down to their younger siblings and cousins.

We'd skated for nearly an hour before I heard a scream and turned to see Billy disappear beneath the ice near a willow bush on the far side of the pond. I was the closest to him and charged toward where the broken ice indicated his point of entry, but saw no sign of him. As I neared the hole, the ice gave way beneath me and

I found myself going under.

As I struggled toward the surface, my hand brushed Billy's coat, I grasped it and kicked my feet hard against the uneven bottom. I thought I heard voices, but saw no one until I felt someone grab him out of my grasp and hoist him to safety. My legs felt heavy and ignored my attempts to get them to move, first numbness came over me, and then a calming peace.

I'll not share with you my theory of death, or what our last moments on earth might be like, but I will share this little Christmas story which flashed across my mind in its entirety as I breathed my last breath. I was, and still am, unclear of what happened afterward, but when I opened my eyes, staring upward, I observed a radiant sterile whiteness all around me. My body seemed to be encompassed by a soft cotton cocoon that gave me no sensory input.

I reasoned that surely I was dead, and in a place where people go before continuing toward heaven. I sensed, rather than heard, a steady repetitive beat akin to, but different than a heart beat. I closed my tired eyes, hoping that when I opened them again, I might see the face of my Savior. Sometime later, when I did open them, the dull noise had been replaced by a sharper and more noticeable beeping, and the face I saw was not Jesus, but the smiling faces of a young man and woman in green scrubs, bending over me.

I will, like all others, someday die, but this Christmas Day was not the day which had been chosen for me. Apparently, there is still much for me to do here on earth before I am called home.

Seeing the Light

The sun's rays seem to bring life to the starkness of the cold winter morning. As I watch the miracle of a new day begin, I stand in awe of the complexity of God's plan.

Jesus describes Himself in scripture as ***the light of the world*** which makes me wonder rather that description is figurative, literal, or possibly both. If He is intelligent energy without form, He could very easily be described as light, IE sunlight; or if He brings to a darkened sinful world hope and truth (light) the statement is likewise true.

There is often a duality of meaning in those things which Jesus describes.

A Little About Me

It was it's warmth which first roused me from slumber, the heat of the sun's rays upon my face, which was poking out of the top of my sleeping bag. Then there was the pleasant brightness of the light that had, hours before, chased away the darkness of the night. Before I had gone to sleep, I had looked heavenward in wonder, and marveled how near the stars seemed in the total darkness of the mountain landscape.

They were so much different than those overhead back in the city, that had to compete with man-made lights of every color and intensity. I had marveled at the stark beauty of the twinkling dots of white against a black background and wondered at man's seeming need to try to usurp God's Majesty. Man has learned nothing it seems, since trying to build the tower of Babel, we cannot **one up** God.

"You awake?" I said, more as a statement than a question, assuming my friend was also awake but unwilling to leave his cozy nest.

"Yeah," John replied. "I'm just enjoying the warmth of the sun. It got cold last night."

I looked around and observed a heavy coat of white frost on everything nearby, including our sleeping bags.

"Down is the only way to go, he said. "All the fancy new man-made fibers can't hold a candle to it."

"Hollow fill is just a copy cat," I answered in agreement. "Just some lab rat trying to earn his pay while imitating God."

We'd been friends as long as I could remember, since early elementary school, when we had moved to the city from the farm. Neither of us had many friends, but as the old saying goes, one good friend is all you need. I'd learned early on the majority of those who claimed friendship would be gossiping about you as soon as you turned your back.

"Are we going to catch our breakfast or cook it from the cooler? "John asked, deferring to me since I usually handled the cooking.

"Some nice crisp **brookies** sound good to me," I answered, referring to the reason we had taken the trip.

The small creek just behind the nearby willows chuckled merrily as it ran over and between ancient rocks, it was teeming with small brook trout, some as large as ten inches, but most between four and six.

"If you'll get a fire going, I'll get our tackle from the car and we'll try our luck," I suggested. "If all else fails, I have a sourdough start in the cooler."

I could see my breath as I rolled from my bag with my Levis still on, and pulled on a sweat shirt and jacket. "Colder than a witch's heart," I commented aloud.

"That's kiss," he corrected, "a witch's kiss."

I ignored him and pulled on wool socks and my hunting boots. By that time John was up and dressing. I walked to the old Ford and began rummaging through the trunk for our fishing gear. I suppose that we were fifteen or sixteen at the time because we both had part-time jobs and rust bucket cars, but had not gone seriously girl crazy yet.

The flicker of a fire had survived long enough to want to feed its hunger for more fuel, when I turned back to our crude camp. John was tediously adding a small twig at a time as the fire struggled to grow. Too little and it would falter and die from lack of fuel, too much and its ability to kindle too much fuel would steal its heat and smother it.

"Some of the bait froze," I commented when I looked into the bait box. Worms are mostly water and do not do well if frozen.

John shook his head but said nothing while he concentrated on the fire. Thirty minutes later we were floating small pieces of earthworm behind an Indiana spinner between the rocks in the small stream and laughing as our efforts were rewarded time and again. Nature provided the fish creel in the form of a forked willow with one side cut on an angle which slipped up through the gills and out the mouth.

The fire, now well established and burning hungrily, accepted our cast iron skillet without complaint and brought it rapidly up to temperature while I dredged the fish in flour and added salt and pepper, before laying them into the greased smoking pan. The fish were small and delicate, when cooked crisp they were eaten hungrily, bones and all while we smiled broadly and commented on our good fortune.

Remembering back now I marvel at how God provided many such memories for us to enjoy in our later years and wonder if John feels the same. When he moved away years ago, we lost contact. I am told he now lives alone and is in poor health, my attempts to reconnect have been unsuccessful. I still miss him a great deal. If God wills, we will have all of eternity to know another again.

~ ~

"There she is!" he yelled, pointing to the young doe that had stopped some fifty yards ahead of us as though waiting for us to catch up.

I stopped running long enough to lever a shell into the chamber of my old 30-30 and fired quickly, just as she resumed bouncing nonchalantly through the pine trees. We were both breathing heavily after following her over several hills, losing ground on the uphill climb only to seemingly gain when we began going downhill again. She was either young and naïve or smart enough to know that we were young and inexperienced, either way she led us on a merry chase for an hour before finally disappearing into a thicket unharmed.

It was a bluebird day in early fall, probably October, and deer season had already been open for some time when we caught a ride to the mountains where John's Dad was working. The area we were hunting was the forested low mountains in the area around Idaho City, Idaho, which has the distinction of being the site of the nation's largest rush gold in the late 1800's. We both knew the area like the back of our hands and couldn't have gotten lost if we'd tried. We were on foot, each with a knap sack of food, and instructions to meet his Dad at a certain place at a given time to secure our ride home.

In the days before outsiders discovered Idaho and moved here, our little paradise was pristine and unsophisticated. Life, of course, as young men was less hurried and carried little responsibility except that which came with being a member of our families. Change is inevitable, but that does not mean we like it.

Thinking back to the book of Exodus and how Israel acted after being freed from slavery in Egypt, I realize that we each want to find a comfortable place and remain there. God kept them moving because He had things to teach them, which could not be learned by sitting by the spring under a palm tree. They had to struggle to find water and food in a harsh land, as do we, to learn the lessons we need in life.

"You missed," he stated the obvious. "You didn't take time to aim before you fired."

Of course, what he had said was true, but I didn't take his criticism well anyway. I replied, "look who's talking, you have missed three shots in a row."

"Where's the game?" John's Dad asked a few hours later, when we arrived at the clearing where he sat in his pickup.

I started to deny we had seen anything but before I could speak, John admitted the truth.

~ ~

The first thing a young man does when he takes ownership of a vehicle is to see how he can improve it over what the manufacturer had engineered. Having done this myself, and watching many of my peers, this seems to me to be a universal truth. We at that point knew hardly anything of the functionality of an automobile but had a need to make it our own, regardless of our skills.

"It's a two-barrel," John said proudly, as though we both knew what that meant. We stood with the hood raised, peering into the engine compartment of his '50 Ford two-door sedan. In the beginning about the only thing we could identify was the battery, but gradually with someone's help, we became conversant with the words plug wires, spark plugs, points, and distributor. It was, like most cars of that vintage, a **three on the tree**, which indicated a three-speed manual transmission as opposed to an automatic or a four-speed which was found then only in trucks and heavier vehicles.

"It's a flat head," I said, having picked up the terminology from my father. I knew all Fords were flat heads until 1954. Only GM products had overhead valves. Both of us had Fords of the same vintage, his was a V8, mine a lowly six.

"I want to get a four-barrel," he declared. "I can really burn the tires with a four-barrel."

Both of us had watched Robert Mitchum in the movie **Thunder Road**. He was a moonshine runner who transported illegal whiskey though the mountains of Tennessee, while being chased by government revenuers. His first vehicle was a hopped up '50 Ford, which after a wreck, was then replaced by a hot '57. I can almost still hear The Ballad of Thunder Road.

There was little doubt that every time we got behind the wheel, we pictured ourselves as Mitchum. He was a "bad good guy" with whom young men could relate. He smoked and greased his black hair adding to his mystique. He also rolled a pack of **cigs** up in the sleeve of his white t-shirt.

Back to our cars, we were soon forced to learn how to change oil, flat tires, and of course spark plugs. Most of the other necessary mechanical work was caused by the way we treated our cars. I learned early on how to pull a transmission and change its syncro rings. This was necessary because I abused the transmission while shifting to second trying to get **scratch**. Nearly any car could get a little scratch from a dead stop in first gear, fewer could get second gear rubber.

With transportation came both freedom and responsibility. The freedom to come and go carried with it the responsibility to maintain the vehicle and feed the few hungry horses living under the hood. Boys, men in training, are fearless and lack good judgment, which is supposed to come later with age. Most learn the hard way by making fatal or nearly fatal mistakes behind the wheel. The devil provides the means to self-destruct in the form of self-indulgences like cigarettes, booze, fast cars, and fast women. God, on the other hand, seems to have a soft heart for fools and protects them from themselves.

Firsts are a big deal for young men – first car, first kiss, first love, etc. Colt 45 was a big deal at the time, first because the name sounded like something a **man** would drink, and secondly because it came in a big can. It is interesting now how such trivial things seemed so important then. As I observe today's generation so much has changed while at the same time so little has really changed.

~ ~

Another of the "firsts" in a young man's life is his first real job. Most of us mowed lawns and shoveled snow in season, or were paid by friends, relatives or neighbors for menial tasks as we were growing up. Our first real jobs, however, involved arriving on time, doing what was required of you, and of course paying taxes on your income. For some, it brought with it the first real taste of responsibility. If you hadn't been taught a work ethic at home by your parents, you were now about to learn one. It also taught you the value of money and how easily it disappeared.

Although I had worked for my uncle at the early age of five, and later in my teens on the farm milking cows for another uncle during the summer, my first real job was working in a body shop sanding cars and readying them for painting. I learned a lot, made a little, and found out right away it was not a trade I wanted to pursue as a career.

In our junior year, three or four of us got on part-time with KFC, which we enjoyed and where we continued to work until after graduation. Graduation from high school is a turning point in their lives for most, some move on and pursue higher education, others careers, while many try to hold on to the past. Looking back now I see many, especially talented athletes, who weren't quite good enough for the big leagues but couldn't let go of the attention they received in high school or college. You can find many of them in bars still today talking about the good old days.

Of our graduating class, some married right away, some served in the military, some pursued a trade, and others made higher education a priority. I see nothing wrong with any of those choices. The only poor choice was not to choose, to stick your head in the sand and pretend you could live at home forever. I call that the **Peter Pan syndrome** and I see many in the current generation choosing it over adulthood.

I chose both, marriage and the US Navy. Looking back now they were the right choices. I wish now, however, I had graduated college before joining the service.

~ ~

We had the better part of a bushel of tomatoes, some green, some ripe, and many which had been frozen and were on the verge of rotting. We had harvested them from John's family garden and were on the prowl. It was Halloween and although we were a little old to go knocking on doors, we were young enough to want to cause a little trouble without really harming anyone.

We stood in the alley behind the houses which lined highway 30, now Fairview Avenue, and watched as cars approached and then lobbed tomatoes over those houses. If our timing was right and our distance correct, we'd splatter an unsuspecting vehicle. Because we could not see them, they could not see us, and we never really knew if we were successful or not.

~ ~

"They've changed the speed limit," I said as we cruised down the new freeway.

When growing up, it had been a two-lane state highway,. When I'd left for Viet Nam it had been widened to four lanes, two running in each direction, with a speed limit of 70 mph. Now, two years later, the speed limit had been reduced to 55.

"Yeah," John replied, "they are trying to control pollution and save on fuel. You have to get a safety inspection every year too."

"For what?" I said in an irritated voice.

"The idea came from the crazies in California and Big Brother threatened to cut federal funding for the highways unless Idaho went along," he answered.

"So, we caved?" I asked incredulously. "Sell your soul to the devil and then he'll pull your strings."

While I'd been gone, our population had doubled and already the influence of the out-of-staters was being felt. Word was that the legislature was already trying to pass a temporary 3% sales tax earmarked for education to accommodate the new resident's children. Education has always been dear to the heart of the voters, so it was sure to pass.

"What else is new? I asked my friend.

"Well..." he said, "Fish & Game have cut the bag limit from 15 fish to 5 fish per day, and we now have separate hunting seasons and tags for bucks and does, archery, and black powder."

"What? You've got to be kidding me!" I said, seeing a glimpse of everything I valued about Idaho change, almost overnight.

A Joni Mitchell song from 1970 comes to mind... "don't it always seem to go that you don't know what you've got 'til it's gone... you paved paradise and put up a parking lot." Maybe our

past and present state leaders could learn something from a lowly song writer.

Mankind, in its arrogance, sees itself as the cause of and solution to all of life's problems. In its efforts to supplant its Creator, it assumes the role of the Creator without the knowledge or ability to do His job. We do not adjust to our environment. we try to adjust the environment to our changing whim. Point in fact: the great Hoover Dam, an engineering miracle, which captures the river to provide electricity and flood control. A good thing? Yes and no. Good from the standpoint of providing electricity to a growing population dependent upon modern conveniences, but bad from the standpoint that the Grand Canyon can no longer purge itself of accumulated silt during the spring run offs and man becomes helpless without electricity. When man intervenes in nature's plan, he sets the law of unintended consequences into play.

Nature, without man's help, will provide per God's design everything needed for the planet to survive until He determines the End of Times has come. By managing forests, wildlife, or resources artificially, we create consequences sometimes worse than the problems we've tried to avoid. My suggestion, spend more time on your knees and less worrying about your carbon footprint.

~ ~

A song from my parent's era had lyrics which many of the young of my generation have unknowingly adopted, "live fast, love hard, die young, and leave a beautiful memory" as I recall. Many did not return from Viet Nam, many others ruined their lives or killed themselves with booze or drugs, and those remaining bear the scars of many battles, both physical and emotional.

Now as I age and the future seems short, the past becomes more important to me. There is hardly anything in the world more painful than seeing the light dim and finally go out in a dear friend's eyes. They remain alive but their soul has moved on. I am finding it difficult to accept the changes and limitations which aging brings. The face in the mirror seems to belong to someone else – I've never been one to accept change gracefully.

~   ~

Seasonally, the canals and ditches that were connected to them designed for irrigation would dry up when the water was shut off in the fall. When that happened, the low spots in those ditches would often be filled with fish of all sizes stranded and waiting to die or be eaten by raccoons or other predators. One such predator was me. Walking the half mile home from the bus stop, I'd often leave the gravel road and investigate the condition of those ditches.

Gerald, a school chum but not what could be called a dear friend, walked home with me one day after school. He, being more of a "city kid" than myself, had to be taught how country life worked. When we came to a large culvert running under the road I stopped and took off my shoes and rolled up my pants, he following my lead. As I now remember, we'd have still been in grade school, maybe fourth or fifth graders. The metal culvert was maybe three to three and a half feet in diameter, forcing us into a half-crouch as we entered. The water remaining on the culvert was less than a foot deep but teemed with fish.

To shorten the story a bit, I'll just say that we caught with our hands one trout 19" and another 21" long, and took them proudly home with us. Some twenty years afterward, his and my paths crossed, and he brought up our adventure as one he'd never forget. I do not know what became of him, but for a short time we enjoyed fellowship that lasted a lifetime.

~ ~

"Hold the muzzle level with the ground, sight down the barrel, center the front bead between the sides of the rear sight," my Dad said. "Now, put the sight under the center of the bull's-eye."

I followed his instructions but had difficulty in holding the rifle steady. I was, give or take, six years old when I bought my used Winchester single shot .22 with the money I 'd earned working for my uncle. .22 shorts were 50¢ for a box of fifty, with longs and long rifles a little more. Dad set up a place where we could shoot safely on our little "acreage" farm, and soon there wasn't a tin can around without holes in it.

My father had grown up on a farm and had later been a sharpshooter and decorated veteran during World War II and was therefore comfortable but respectful of weapons. To my great pleasure, he and I would occasionally go to the nearby desert and help Mother Nature control the jack rabbit population, much to the delight of the hawks, eagles, coyotes, and other predators, I'm sure.

In that day, one could get a license to hunt big game at age twelve, and I did. I'd worked the summer before and purchased a used Winchester 30-30 lever action and was eager to try it out. At that time, it was the only big game rifle our family owned. When the season opened, I remember Dad showing me how to move through the terrain quietly, carefully placing my feet so as to not make noise, and how to be constantly vigilant of my surroundings. He hunted slowly and methodically, I of course, always gauged my activity by the number of miles I put on my boots. We had little extra money to spend for sport and therefore balanced the cost of the hunt with the potential to supplement our family's diet with fresh meat.

We parked the vehicle nearly at the summit of Bald Mountain

which meant nearly any game found would be found below us. I do not recommend this as a regular practice, but there was no road access below us so we did. The day was nippy when we unloaded from the old Ford, but weather was clear and it warmed up as the day progressed. An hour or two into the hunt we'd dropped about a third of the way down the mountain and were "side-hilling" through pine, fir, and aspen trees when Dad stopped and held his finger to his lips indicating that I should be quiet.

He whispered, "there's a leaf up there that doesn't look right." He pointed toward a thicket of aspen trees ahead and slightly uphill from our location.

I remember scampering up on a big granite boulder. What I could see clearly from my vantage point was a bull elk lying down with his head and antlers visible. I raised my rifle and pulled the trigger. Minutes later we were field dressing a nice yearling bull. I quote my Dad, "now the work begins."

Dad was in his mid-forties at the time and weighed something around 145. Each quarter was about a hundred pounds and the vehicle was uphill maybe a half mile. You gotta figure what kind of a man could make four trips up and down hill with a hundred pounds on his back. In those days they called it **grit or sand**. I still stand in awe of him. No one was ever prouder of his son than my Dad, who took every opportunity to recount how I killed my first elk with a single shot to the head.

~ ~

The last elk I shot, and likely the last one I'll ever shoot, was the day my first granddaughter Nicole was born. My best friend Mark and I were on a draw hunt in eastern Idaho. I had drawn a tag, but he had not, however the area was familiar to him because his wife's family lived there. So, in essence, he was my guide as well as companion.

I was carrying the 300 Winchester magnum my lovely wife had traded an old boat for years before. It has the distinction that it has never failed to drop its game in a single shot. It was a nice fall day and we had risen early and were on the mountain following a road which was closed to motorized traffic. We'd hunted together many times shooting ducks, geese, pheasants, and quail, but never elk. With the changing climate in Fish & Game, hunters not only had to plan their hunts far in advance, but also decide what sex, antler count, and weapon they wanted to use. It was also certainly not a given that all members of a group of hunters would be lucky enough to "draw" together.

We were in "big" country, on mountains seemingly from some old western where everything was larger than life. With thousands of feet of mountain above us and a few thousand below we could see for miles across the valley, through which the Lemhi river ran.

I'm not sure, but I think it was my guide Mark who first saw the herd of elk below us making their way upward toward our location. They seemed to have been spooked and were heading uphill fast in a long line, maybe twenty or thirty in the herd. I remembering seeing a nice bull coming our way and waited until he got within range to fire. Rather than falling, he swung around and headed back into the trees the way he had come.

"You missed!" Mark exclaimed in amazement.

I did not have time to argue or make excuse because in reality there was no excuse for missing such an easy shot. We turned our attention to the herd that was still coming our way in spite of my shot, and waited. A larger bull came across the road on which we were standing and I dropped him with a heart shot. When we got to him, he seemed as big as a horse.

"You start gutting him and I'll go back to the ranch and get a horse," Mark said. The family ranch was a few miles downhill from where we had been forced to park our pickup. He left and I began to try and manage the unmanageable carcass by myself. I had used rope to tie it off to nearby brush to hold it open, and just as I began the awesome task two hunters arrived, complemented me and asked about others. I shared the fact that the majority of the herd had gone uphill but I had missed a bull that had gone down.

I continue my story now only because the statute of limitations on stupidity has ran out. My granddaughter is now 26.

I had opened up the animal and rolled out the guts when my earlier visitors returned and stated, "you're a better shot than you thought."

I knew I was in trouble and tried to work my way out by offering them the bull but they thanked me and refused, saying they wanted to shoot their own. I tried to cover myself by lying and telling them that my hunting partner had gone back to get horses and would tag the animal when he returned, hoping that they would say nothing to anyone. When Mark returned, he had two horses and his sister-in-law who did indeed have a legal tag and took the extra animal.

We were back at the ranch skinning the animals when a phone call advised me I was a grandfather. I left for Boise post haste. The locker meat alone from my bull was nearly a thousand pounds. The elk mount hung on my wall for many years until we moved to a home that had no room for it. I'd hoped to give it to Nicole but that never quite worked out.

Whether completely true or not, my stories are true and complete as I remember and savor each of them.

~ ~

We, seven of us, had gone down in our jet boat into Hells Canyon to fish and spend the weekend, as I often did. This time however, my passengers were not the seasoned *fisher buddies* who often accompanied me. This time I had my wife, her brother and sister-in-law, my wife's aunt, and my oldest daughter and her husband; all of which were greenhorns when it came to running big whitewater. Our youngest daughter and boyfriend didn't come down until the next day.

For those who don't know, it is always the operator (captain's) responsibility to make sure everything goes well and no one gets hurt. That made it incumbent on me to remember, have, and load everything the party may need while we were there. Nothing can be forgotten or left at home because there is nowhere to get anything, you must be totally self-sufficient.

Also true is that this was an exceptionally large crew for our 22' boat. Tents, sleeping bags, food, drink, cookware, tackle, bait, toiletries, water and clothing for nearly a dozen people for three days filled the boat. I had to make two trips downstream, the first with the gear and the second to shuttle the passengers. It should have been a clue right then that we needed a second jet boat.

I unloaded the gear and returned and loaded the passengers. We were riding low in the water with no surplus of horsepower to navigate the bigger rapids. I was familiar with the river but because it fluctuates in its flow a great deal daily, it is never quite the same. I've been there at 6500 feet per second and at 35,000 feet. Rocks very evident at low water are sometimes barely under the surface when it rises.

We arrived at camp safely, set up the tents, laid out our bedding, made a fire pit and set up the kitchen. Several were eager to wet their lines and harvest the promised fish so I took them to several of my favorite spots. Fishing was good so when we returned to camp, a second group was ready to try their luck. I do not recall what I dutch-ovened but do remember everyone went to bed full and happy. It was during the summer months, which made the canyon feel very hot and dry, without any breeze.

After breakfast the next morning, I went back upstream to pick up Tammi and Mike, her boyfriend, to have them join us. Going down I made a critical error, letting the boat get away from the rocks and onto a shallow portion in the center of the river. As I heard the small rocks hit the bottom, I should have hit the gas and gotten on top of the water. I did not, instead I cut the throttle and the boat lowered until it rested on the gravel bar. As the passing water spun the boat sidewise, the jet nozzle caught on a rock and cracked its casing. We made it back downstream to camp but had little power and no control of the boat.

Picture the boat tied up along the rocky shoreline, me in the water to my chest trying to determine the problem. I finally felt the ragged edges of the broken aluminum casing and knew there was no repair that I could do there. I removed the nozzle and caught a ride upstream to the boat landing, where I made a phone call to a friend who agreed to get a new nozzle and meet me half way.

I caught a ride back to camp late that afternoon and was struggling to install the new nozzle when my wife yelled, "there's a rattlesnake!"

I tried to ignore her and finish the repair, without success. I go out of the water just in time to see my sister-in-law running toward the boat, a .357 swinging back and forth in her hands, ready to shoot into the rocks where the snake was. That was way more frightening than the snake, which I killed with a shovel.

~ ~

I told you Dad was from a farming background. I remember him jokingly saying as we drove by farms and ranches, "you can tell who wears the pants in that family." Which, of course, always begged the reply, "how?

He'd just laugh and say, "if the barn is bigger than the house, it is the man, if the house is bigger than the barn, it is the woman."

I have my own version which goes, "I wear the pants in my family, she just tells me which pair to put on."

~ ~

I told you earlier that God protects the young and the foolish. I live today as a testimony of that truth. It was the summer of 1966, my wife and I had already set a date for an August wedding. As some young men do, I felt the need to act stupid while I still had the chance, before I settled down to the married life. My friend Dick and I drove the few short miles to a nearby reservoir called Lucky Peak, although one may or may not argue if the trip was lucky for me. Like everything in my early days, it involved poor judgment and beer.

We spent the day soaking up the sun on the beach by the water and drinking beer before heading back toward town. Looking back, I must have had a guilty conscience because I wrongly assumed the driver of the *official* vehicle following me from the swimming area somehow knew I was drunk and underage. Traffic coming home from a weekend in the mountains was slow and bumper to bumper, which forced this impatient young man at first opportunity, to put the pedal to the metal and lay on the horn as I passed several vehicles.

Unfortunately, as I tried to regain my lane, I found myself in the middle of a turn. It didn't end well when I over corrected and rolled the car several times into a hay field beside the road. Dick was thrown clear and my leg was pinned underneath the car outside, with the door partly closed on it, when the crowd from a nearby bar arrived at the scene. Except for the Lord's grace I should have lost or broken my leg, or died. I have a sizeable scar on that leg still to remind me that I was spared.

A couple of days in the hospital, several weeks on crutches trying to dismantle my totaled car, and our wedding day postponed for a couple of months was the result. I lost my license and received a fine for reckless driving for my trouble. Dick, who at first seemed to be hurt the most, was not seriously injured and recovered in time to be my best man. "Stupid is as stupid does..." to quote Forrest Gump.

~ ~

One winter when we were still young and foolish, my friend John and his wife joined me and my wife for a trip to the mountains to go tubing. When we arrived, we found the hill closed because the snow had melted and refrozen to ice, making it too dangerous for the business to operate safely. The proprietor told us if we used the hill, we were on our own. We had our own tubes, the energy to climb the hill, but lacked the common sense to return home.

I don't remember if I heard "no" or "go" from my friend just prior to pushing off down the slope. Two on a big tube, we hit a bump and went airborne before crashing and burning on the icy ground.

Back in town at the ER a short time later, they checked Marsha for a concussion and me for a separated shoulder. The young are resilient but not very smart.

~ ~

We had just bought a big, new, class A motor home when we

and our neighbors, Mark and Mary, made the decision to pull the Bayliner behind it and go crappie fishing. Since it was the maiden voyage a new bottle of amber liquid joined us. We were ten years older now and had two children each but had not gained a bit in the way of common sense or good judgment.

The little reservoir was just across the state line into Oregon and was well known for great crappie fishing. The summer day was hot as both the booze and miles fell behind us. By the time we arrived, loaded our gear aboard, and launched the boat, life was good among friends. The boat was a fiberglass ski boat, so to make it usable, the top was folded down to give us each access to the lake, as we drifted looking for schools of fish.

If you haven't fished for them, let me describe how it works. Very light gear and line with a variety of small rubber jigs with hooks in them are used, some fishermen add a kernel of white corn to the hook, many do not. The key to success is to find a school of fish, judge their depth, jig the bait up and down, while trying different colors and designs until you begin to get strikes. The little sun fish are not bashful, if they like what they see, they eat it. It is similar to bass fishing, but with less wary prey.

If you can picture the four of us all casting, jigging, and retrieving on different sides of the boat at the same time, you have a clear picture. Add to the fact we were in the hot sun, well-oiled by alcohol, so any sane person could smell disaster in the making. None were aboard.

My shirt was off and I was facing 180º from Mark when it happened. On his cast, the bass jig he had been using hung up in my back, just above the kidney. He attempted to cast twice more before I yelled, "you've got me!" By that time the hook was well set into the muscle. Ironically, it neither hurt nor bled.

The three of them appraised the situation and spoke of leaving and going to the hospital but I nixed the idea and suggested that a sharp filet knife and a steady hand could extract it so we could resume fishing. Neither Marsha nor Mark was up for the challenge but Mary agreed to try and cut alongside of the hook so we could remove it. I must have winced or moved as she cut because she refused to continue.

Once back at camp, we tried to cut the large treble hook off without success and my helpers were not willing to continue. When I suggested that maybe someone at the lodge would have the ability to remove it Mark agreed to go. He returned from the bar with a big, rough looking guy who agreed to pull it out with pliers if I was up for it. I remember lying face down on the couch with him over me. He lifted my torso off the couch before the hook finally gave up the ghost and pulled free. A single Band-Aid covered the wound and I was on my feet immediately getting ready to cook dinner for us.

None of my crew had an appetite after watching the events transpire. I don't recall much after that about the rest of the fishing trip or the trip home the next day, but will never forget being **hooked up**.

~ ~

And then there was the time… Sorry folks, I had to use it somewhere.

We, Doug, Jerry, and I, had planned for the better part of a year a trip to go fishing on Vancouver Island in British Columbia. Doug is my brother-in-law who lives in Alaska, and Jerry was once my boss who became my friend. Doug knows fishing but little about boats, Jerry knows little about either but was up for the adventure. I read and studied everything I could about salmon and halibut fishing, which was touted in the area of Campbell River. I owned a 22-foot inboard jet and lots of heavy tackle but had no experience navigating in the ocean, except time on a ship in the Navy.

For the trip, I had purchased one of the first civilian GPS units in the event we needed to return to land, but had no clue of where it was. My compass was only as good as my ability to read charts and that was poor.

If I can paint an accurate picture, we left Boise in my one ton dually, pulling a boat filled with gear and weighing 6000 pounds. Our route took us to Oregon, then north through Washington past Seattle and north again into Canada. We stopped only to fuel and change drivers, with the shotgun taking the wheel and the driver retiring to the back seat to rest. We arrived at the ferry about midnight, just in time to make the last one of the day. When we arrived on the island, we were dead tired, with Campbell River still a hundred miles to the north. We pulled to the side of the road and went to sleep, waking to the sound of passing traffic. Day two began with high hopes, as we set out toward our destination.

It seemed like forever, as it always does when you are eager to arrive somewhere, but finally the sign announced the little town on the water. We asked where boats where launched, bought our permits, and continued to a little park where we set up our tents, arranged our kitchen, and prepared for an early departure the next morning. The weather was overcast and threatened rain so I erected a little tent over my cook stove. Both of my compatriots enjoy their beer and found comfortable lawn chairs, while I began to cook.

Monsoon time, I kid you not, the worst rainstorm I'd ever seen, began falling and continued into the night. We took shelter in the covered boat and ate our meal there while rain beat on the roof. The tent did its job in spite of the downpour and kept our sleeping bags dry, allowing us to catch some sleep before time to eat and launch the boat.

Day three, we enjoyed a quick breakfast and cups of coffee before backing the boat into the salty water, with high hopes. I should have paid more attention to the low tide and the huge amount of debris in the water. With all its strengths and horse-power, a jet boat relies upon gathering a large volume of water into the pump before reducing it at the nozzle, to provide steering and propulsion. Our pump was immediately clogged with sea-weed and kelp, rendering us nearly helpless.

After vain attempts to clear it without success, I used my new marine radio to call the Coast Guard. Embarrassingly, when they came to our rescue, we were only a couple hundred feet from the boat launch. Day three ended with me feeling foolish, with little heart to put the boat back into the water. We went to town to get a tide chart and ended up in a local pub, hearing from the locals that last night's storm was the worst in twenty years. The pints, as they call them in Canada, went down easily as we planned the strategy for the next day.

Day four, we launched at high tide without difficulty, while paying special attention to floating seaweed. This would have been about August 13th, a few days after my birthday. Beautiful day, calm seas, wonderful surroundings, with high expectations as we made our way slowly between the islands. We caught several smaller fish but nothing like we had hoped for. In the afternoon, having lost my crab pot and only boating two keepers, we decided to return to town and have lunch.

We came into the breakwater and tied up the boat within

eyesight of a seaside restaurant that promised great seafood stew. Sitting on an open deck overlooking the water, we began to eat before one of my friends remarked, "look, there's a boat just like yours."

Sadly, it was not a boat just like mine, it was mine and was rapidly leaving the area at full throttle. Hours later, after the Coast Guard had retrieved it, we learned that two local drunks well known to the RCMP had taken it and ran it out of fuel before being captured, but not before losing or breaking hundreds of dollars of equipment. I called home only to find that a dear friend had died on my birthday days before. That ended our adventure.

We returned home the following morning, our boat damaged, and our hopes for success crushed. After repeated calls to try and get restitution for my financial losses, I found they were given thirty days and released without further responsibility.

~   ~

Thirty and more years ago when we were younger and more social, we began a monthly poker party. The original idea, since we were all young, poor, and still raising families, was to have the host couple furnish the main dish and their guests bring snacks and their own choice of beverages. Initially, there was between six and ten couples who regularly participated. Since it was penny anté, a big night was to win or lose $20, with most of us staying in the $10 range.

At the end of the first year the food thing had gotten way out of control, with every couple trying one-up the cuisine of the previous host. It had gone the gambit from chili and corn bread to prime rib with all the fixin's. We all found it hard to reign in the menu when it became a competition.

My memory takes me back to a particular night when we

were the hosts and I was pranked by my good friend Chuck, who was a well-known jokester. About midway through the evening something came up in the conversation regarding walnuts. I do not recall why but he said the word walnuts in an odd way that made me respond, "you sound like a hair-lip."

He didn't answer but instead excused himself to use the restroom and while he was gone, his wife asked in front of everyone, "don't you know he has a hair-lip?"

Since I had first met him, he'd always worn a little scraggly mustache with what appeared to be missing hairs in the center; now I immediately put two and two together and felt lower than dirt at my thoughtless ridicule. But of course, unknown to me, they had planned the trick well in advance and let me bleed at the poker table for a while before laughing and telling me the truth.

A different time, I left the table and someone dropped a folded up twenty under my chair while I was gone. The whole table waited for my return to see how I would handle it. I handled it poorly, knowing that if I asked, everyone would try to claim it, so I slipped it into my pocket while trying to decide how to handle my new-found wealth. Boo... wrong thing to do. Everyone was on me like I'd killed a kitten, accusing me of being a thief before then getting another good laugh at my expense. Gradually the poker group disbanded, with each of us going their own way. but still staying friends.

~   ~

As we left the small town of Council, Idaho, and headed up into the mountains toward Hells Canyon, my wife and I, with another couple, were in search of firewood. Our Ford F250 was pulling a small two-wheeled utility trailer in the hopes that each family could go home with a nice cord of dry firewood.

As I remember, it was a late summer, with the morning sun just beginning to take the chill off the high mountain air. This was still in the days before stretch and extra cabs, therefore the four of us were packed four across into the seat. As we proceeded uphill, we kept lookout for dry standing trees close to the road on the uphill side. Anyone who has ever harvested firewood knows carrying wood uphill to the truck is time and energy wasted. The road, a single track with a sprinkling of gravel over dirt, wound upward at a leisurely rate, making the ride pleasant.

In an instant that all changed, the road ahead was filled with the front end of a Kenworth coming toward us, going downhill empty. Neither of us had the option to stop, and the road was too narrow for us to pass. All I can remember now is the sound of his Jake brake and my reflex to turn the wheel hard to the right, toward the mountainside. Turning left would have taken us downhill into the canyon.

By God's grace, the hillside had been cut away at a forty-five which acted like a super on a racetrack. We went up and then back down in a second, as I turned the wheel hard to the left, just as the semi passed by. He never slowed or came back to see what happened to us. We stopped in the center of the road in shock, as we realized that nothing was damaged and no one hurt. We could have easily died that day. I have no recollection of firewood.

~ ~

We have two daughters, Teresa the oldest, and Tamara her younger sister. They are both married and now pushing fifty years old, and each has a daughter of their own. Terri was conceived while we were still in the Navy but delivered after they gave us an **early out**, thus making it our responsibility to cover the ensuing medicals. Lesson learned, everything which seems good is not and often has a downside. Tammi was born about three years later.

Both my wife and I grew up in homes slightly above the poverty level and because of this we had a hunger for those things we thought we lacked. Society is quick to fuel your hunger, always offering you more, newer, and bigger. I marvel now at the size of things, especially drink and food items. It's little wonder the American public look by-in-large like hippos, in spite of fad diets and burgeoning health and fitness clubs, with personal trainers. A television commercial for orange juice summed it up nicely. A woman's personal trainer was exercising for her while she watched, doing nothing.

I grew up believing, and still do, that ambition was a good thing; that a good work ethic and hard work was the answer to having anything we wanted. I have found, however, that this assumption is both right and wrong. One reason for its failure is man's propensity to never quite be happy with what he has, the other is that life does not treat our efforts equally. Conversely, rarely does one succeed without trying, it is essential that we commit ourselves if we desire success.

We had our first home built in 1970 and moved to our second in 1976. Our third was completed in 1990 and after living there a half-dozen years, elected to build in the mountains. That construction was delayed, forcing us to purchase yet another while it was under construction. We moved into our dream home in the nearby mountains in 2000, returning to town in 2005, ironically into a used home just blocks from the one we had left.

We stayed there until moving to our current one, about eight years later. The whole point of this dialogue is to show that during the course of our 50+ years together, we have constantly searched for the answer to our discontentment. I could list the more than one hundred vehicles we have owed, but will not do so. We spent our retirement and kid's inheritance looking for something. Suffice to say that neither wealth, nor things, bring lasting happiness, only Jesus offers contentment.

As the end of our earthly lives fast approaches. the 'woulda', 'coulda', 'shouldas' are many... but the opportunities to make changes to the past do not exist, and never did. Attempts to teach others from our mistakes are usually unsuccessful and not appreciated, therefore we try and remain content with the knowledge that we are growing in our faith and maturity.

The Tempest

A tempest is a storm; it most often refers to one at sea, which is also called a squall. The tempests in our lives, like those in nature, often arise suddenly and without warning, leaving us without time to make preparation. In those times and others seeming less urgent, we are powerless, hopeless, and fearful. Few, even most who do not recognize God as our Creator, turn to Him only in the moment of their greatest need. I was Navy, not Army or Marines, but still understand the meaning of the old saying "there are no atheists in a foxhole."

If it was not so sad, it would be amusing to watch a big strong presumably self-made man, finally give up his battle with pride and turn to God after all else had failed. God wants us humble ourselves and be dependent upon Him, but I believe He seldom "breaks" us Himself; He lets our poor decisions lead us to where we break ourselves.

Have you watched a seemingly happy marriage fall apart, financial success disappear, or health issues destroy our illusion of independence? Only in those times, when we come to the end of ourselves, can we truly embrace God and stop trying to compete with Him.

~   ~

They liked the same music, enjoyed the same foods, shared many of the same dreams for the future, and that was the basis on which they hoped to build a happy life together. It was simplistic and naïve of course, but such is the way of the young, who make their decisions based almost solely on their emotions. To their parents credit, they began life with a good value system, meaning that they were willing to work for what they wanted to achieve; rather than expecting it to be given to them.

I see now that the poor have the distinct advantage over the rich, in that they are forced to learn the value of things, and in doing so, appreciate them more. Additionally, they have experience in making ends meet and thus, when faced with future financial problems, will have experience in working through the crisis, where the "silver spooners" will not.

~ ~

"Are you going to college? she asked, as we sat in my old car finishing our Mickey D's lunch, before returning to school.

"My parents want me to, I answered. "But they can't afford to send me and I've been too lazy to work hard enough to get a scholarship."

"Mine too," she agreed, "but I'm not sure what I'd study if I did go, I envy those kids who already know what they want to do in life."

I finished my Big Mac, started the car, smiled at her and said, "you've got catsup on your chin."

She gave me a petulant frown, wiped her chin with a napkin, then smiled and gave me a peck on the cheek as she grasped my elbow and pulled it to her possessively. We had, at that point, never discussed marriage, I think both of us just assumed it was a natural extension of our relationship that would happen when the time was right. With only four months until graduation, it bothered me that I still had a **kid job** which paid just enough for gas and dates, but wouldn't come close to covering the costs of food and housing. I made a mental note to begin trying to find something that would work into a career.

Career Day is the day set aside for the senior class to meet with some of the local businessmen and women, and seriously consider what many had to that point, not made any attempt to do. Professionals of every sort, from universities, to blue collar recruiters for the trades, and the military, were all there. Each of them presented a favorable view of why young men and women may want to consider what they pitched.

Eva, to my surprise, immediately took a special interest in education, and I liked what I heard from the Navy recruiter about defending our country and learning a skill which would pay well later in private life. I, of course, saw myself as a fighter pilot, which the recruiter was quick to point out, required a college education. No one is going to put a high school kid behind the wheel of a multi-million dollar aircraft. I was disappointed, but still interested. Eva, on the other hand, was already committed to making a serious attempt at getting a teaching certificate, regardless of the financial hardships involved.

My GPA, at a 3.6 was, I knew, a result of my God-given gifts, not of my commitment to education, but it was good enough for the recruiter to offer me financial assistance in return for making a six-year commitment. I promised to speak with my parents and get back to him, but he made a counter offer – he a set date to come to my house and present the program directly to my parents himself. I guess he'd heard *"I'll get back to ya"* before.

As I drove Eva home, we talked excitedly about the direction our lives seemed to be taking, but not about how it may affect our future together. Eva's grandmother matched the small scholarship given to her by our church, and she ratcheted up her efforts to find a part time job. After a lengthy conversation, most of which was to convince my mother that her son had become a man, I signed the papers which would assure me financial assistance at the Naval academy. All that remained then was a congressional sponsor, which God soon provided. Equal parts of apprehension and excitement were alternately a very real part of each day, as the school year came to an end and our graduation became real.

It as Eva who put what we had both been thinking into words. "What about us?" she asked, as we stood in line waiting for tickets at the movie theater. I remember trying hard to come up with a reassuring answer to the question that had also been on my mind for several weeks, but failed.

"I'm not sure," I finally answered truthfully. "Maybe we should commit to waiting to see how the first year goes before making a decision."

She gave my arm her usual little squeeze, smiled at me and said, "that's just what I was thinking."

I surprised myself at the Academy, I immediately adopted a better work ethic and study habits. Maybe, just maybe, I was beginning to mature and take life seriously, or just possibly with my social life now a zero, there was nothing to distract me. In the beginning Eva and I spoke daily, but as our studies became more difficult, we found that Saturday and one evening during the week was enough to keep each other up-to date on the events occurring in our lives.

Except for classes, I seldom left my dorm room, other than to eat and go to the library. From her accounts, Eva was doing much the same. Time seemed to go by quickly now that we had each committed ourselves to a goal.

We had graduated high school in 1983, now four years later we found ourselves graduating once again, only this time from a university. We had spent the holidays, spring breaks, and Christmas enjoying our time together, but were soon aware both we and our relationship had changed. We'd never been intimate but had steamed up our share of car windows over the course of the six years we'd known one another, always stopping before stepping over the line.

As she began her first year as a school teacher, I entered flight school and began the training which I hoped would ultimately put me on the deck of an aircraft carrier. Always a thousand miles and more apart, our calls became less and less frequent, and our relationship became almost platonic. I had my commission and she her career, when I got my orders to report to the USS Ranger CV61, which was operating in the Middle East as a part of a new operation called Desert Storm – the date was January of 1991.

I'm not sure what I had expected, but the harsh realities of life soon made themselves very apparent to me. Even the mundane routines carried with them the reality that life and death were but different sides of the same coin. My wing commander was Commander Davis, he had served in Viet Nam on the USS Enterprise CVN65, the first nuclear carrier. He was only days short of his 30 and retirement, when he was shot down and killed in Iraq by some low-tech weapon, operated by a towel-head with little training.

I flew mission after mission, watching as my munitions rained death down from the sky and felt a sense of satisfaction, knowing that the enemy was paying dearly for the atrocities exacted against those whom we considered allies.

Good guys versus bad guys, Christians versus heathens, that war has lasted since time began – only the names, faces, and weaponry change. Alone at night, I reasoned that this was no more than an extension of the Crusades. I was not oblivious to the fact that this war was also about access to cheap oil and the testing of sophisticated weaponry under combat conditions which would allow Congress to justify spending additional billions on future weapons.

We stood off the coast and out of range of short-range weapons, surrounded by escorts and destroyers, whose charge it was to handle anything incoming from the coast before it got to the carrier. Rockets, planes, or even high-powered boats laden with explosives suited the mindset of the suicidal enemy, who lacked serious armament.

~   ~

School had just begun and with it my third year as a teacher. Except when the evening news caught my attention, I had little time to think about Jack or the war raging in the Middle East. My focus was on the 28 third-graders who had been put in my care, and of juggling my lackluster personal life with my commitment to them. Teaching consumed my life, I suppose because I let it, and also because it was the only thing I had ever made a firm commitment to. On several occasions I was asked out, but mostly only by co-workers or some obviously married man separated from his wife and looking for something I was not.

As word of the end of the war broke, I remember taking time to sit down and write Jack a long letter and feeling guilty because it had been so long since I'd last written. I finally poured my heart out to him.

~ ~

I couldn't remember feeling more excited when I opened
Eva's letter and began to read. First there was guilt, then a sense
of loneliness filled my heart, and I was forced to come to terms
with the fact that I still loved her. Although the war was officially
over and some of my peers were being given leave, our ship
remained on station and continued to provide air support for the
troops on the ground, as they began to withdraw. I remember
now the dubious distinction of being one of only 36 US aircraft
shot down during the short war.

Our mission was routine by normal standards, with only two
A6 Intruders launched and tasked to observe and protect our
troops on the ground. We had been given a defensive role and
had orders to fire only when fired upon. Iraq's meager air force
had, by that time, already been destroyed and posed little or no
threat and what remained of their SCUD missiles were unsophisticated and ineffective when used as surface to air. Word on the
ship was that we'd be heading stateside by the end of the month,
where it was likely that the ship would be decommissioned.

We were flying at 10,000 feet when the squawk came in.
Below us, hidden in a sandstorm, two enemy tanks had a convoy
of our men pinned down and they had requested our assistance.
I followed my lead man down, coming in low and fast, relying on
our air to surface missiles to handle the threat with little difficulty. As I look back now, I realize that Goliath was killed by a
rock because he let his pride get in the way of caution.

Although both tanks were reduced to piles of smoking ruin,
within seconds, a single man with a SAM sent it right up my tail
pipe as I flew by. I bailed out, too low for my chute to deploy, but

too high to hit the sand without injury. By the time the other plane realized I'd been hit and circled back, the blowing sand had erased any trace of me and my captors had already loaded me into a truck, headed to their headquarters.

At first, I thought my back was broken, the pain was excruciating and I was unable to stand as I was dragged from the truck and thrown on the floor of a locked enclosure. I was stripped of my flight suit and boots, and beaten. Mercifully, at some point I blacked out. Unknown to me, my ELD (electronic location device) had been found still attached to the ejection seat and ground troops were combing the area unsuccessfully, trying to find me.

When I awakened, it was night, the acrid smell of the smoke of burning rubber assaulted my nostrils. Somewhere outside of my confinement, armed men were cooking over a fire fueled by a burning tire. I could hear them laughing and talking clearly, but could not understand anything but an occasional reference to "American" which I assumed was me. From time to time during the night, one or several of them would enter, kick me a few times and leave laughing. I was now so thirsty the beatings were almost a welcome distraction from the pain of my thirst.

Once during the night, I heard the familiar sound of a Huey flying overhead, which fueled my hope of a rescue that did not happen. It was light when the door opened and several men entered, one in a ragged uniform. I noted that the others deferred to him in a way that gave me reason to believe he was in charge. He kicked me once in the ribs to make sure I was awake, spat on the ground, and uttered the single word, **infidel**, before leaving.

~   ~

I was grading papers at home while waiting for my left-overs to heat in the microwave when the phone rang. It was Jack's mother, and she was in tears.

"Jack's plane has been shot down," Gladys sobbed. "They don't know if he is alive or dead."

"I'll come right over," I said as I stood and reached for my coat.

Jack's father had died just weeks before, leaving her lost and alone. At his funeral, she had looked and acted so broken that I could only imagine what the news had done to her fragile psyche. As I drove, I prayed for both her and for Jack's safety, while realizing as I did, how very much he still meant to me. When I arrived, she was waiting on the porch and immediately melted into my arms.

At her request, I spent the night after returning home to get some clothes and my briefcase. When she finally went to sleep, I finished grading papers, before passing out on the couch from fatigue. *The circle is getting smaller* a voice in my head said, which I took to mean that life is both short and uncertain. When I had started my first year as a teacher, both of my parents were alive, as were Jack and his parents. Now it was just Gladys and I, and hopefully Jack. My Mom and Dad had died instantly, the officer said, when a drunk had crossed over the center line and hit them head on.

A week, and then two went by with no word about Jack.

~   ~

By my count. it had been thirteen days since I had been captured, and more since I'd had a decent meal. I was given a single canteen of dirty water each morning with what appeared to be the left-over scraps from my captor's meal of the previous night. Any attempt to get more was rewarded by the toe of a boot.

The uniformed man, I found, spoke English quite well and seemed to take pride in that fact, as he repeated it aloud over and over, as if to remind himself. "I speak good English," he'd say, before trying to interrogate me. My back still ached and there was a numbness in both legs, however in spite of it, I was able to stand and move about when I was alone. I wanted them to believe I had no mobility in the event they were careless enough to give me a chance to escape.

That evening, two of the men entered the room carrying a makeshift litter made from wooden crates, while a third held his AK at the ready in the event I would try to escape. I was thrown on it and carried outside where I got the first look at my surroundings in the dim light. It appeared that my prison was the only structure in the area and that a large, man-made cave nearby housed the combatants and their equipment. Brush and weeds had been placed on the roof of the house and would, no doubt, make it invisible from the air unless searchers used thermo imaging.

"Are you a Christian?" the uniformed man asked, almost pleasantly.

He'd caught me so off guard that I answered without thinking. "Yes," I said.

"You'll renounce your Jesus and accept Allah as the one true God or you will die," he screamed, while brandishing a wicked looking sword.

I remained silent and received a blow to the side of my head with the flat of his sword for my trouble. The desert landscape spun before me and I fought to stay conscious as second and third blows of like kind hit me. "Lord give me strength to endure," I prayed, knowing my resolve was weak. Almost immediately a strange look came over my attacker's face before he suddenly turned and walked away, leaving me surrounded by slack-faced heathens, who looked almost hypnotized.

I struggled to my feet, watching them warily. None of them moved or showed an interest in me, almost as if I had disappeared. I walked briskly from the circle and out of camp into the night. As I walked, the pain in my back seemed to diminish and my resolve to live grew with each successive step. I do not know how long I walked, it seemed like hours.

For some reason I imagined my position south of where the plane went down, so I followed the North Star to keep me from wandering in circles. Bits of two scriptures filled my head as I walked and pondered what had taken place. The first was when Peter had been arrested and imprisoned and an angel came and released him. The second, different but much like it, was when the crowds were going to throw Jesus from the cliff and He just walked through them and left them standing there.

"Halt or I'll shoot!" someone suddenly barked from the darkness. "Identify yourself."

"Lieutenant Jack Hastings, US Navy" I answered quickly, before giving my service number.

"Hastings of the Ranger?" an excited voice asked. "The flyboy who got shot down?"

"The same," I smiled, knowing that I was finally safe.

Instantly from the darkness, three young men in desert camo appeared with broad grins across their faces. "Welcome home lieutenant," the first one said, extending his hand.

I was driven back to their camp in a Humvee and within the hour was returned to my ship by a medivac chopper. X-rays confirmed that severe trauma to my spine caused by impact had damaged several discs, which disqualified me from returning to duty.

~   ~

When Gladys received word of Jack's rescue, I was her first call. "Jack has been found," she beamed. "He's coming home!"

"Is he alright" I asked her, worrying that he'd been injured.

"He said he was fine," she answered, "but they won't let him return to flying."

The caveat at the end of her sentence bothered me but I said nothing, fearing I might further worry her.

It was nearly a month before we actually watched Jack walk off the plane and down the ramp. Apparently, he had spent time in Germany at a medical facility before going to Walter Reed and receiving a medical discharge. I had not seen him in nearly three years and during those years, he seemed to have aged ten. In my mind I still pictured him as a skinny kid walking across the gym floor to accept his diploma and what I now saw was a man, rapidly nearing 30, who had painful experiences of life etched into his handsome face.

Jack bent and took his mother in his arms, looked around as though somehow expecting to see his Dad before remembering he was gone, then smiled and hugged me off the ground, before giving me a full-on kiss on the lips. We live in a small town where the word of his return had gotten out, and a dozen or more of the locals stood waiting patiently for their turn to greet their home-town hero.

"Hungry?" I asked after I had gotten behind the wheel of Gladys' big Buick.

"Starving," Jack answered smiling. "The airline sold me a soggy, two-day-old tuna sandwich for five bucks and a can of warm coke for two."

"Burger Den?" I asked almost automatically, "or McDonald's?"

Gladys frowned, probably thinking a big fancy celebration dinner was more in order, but said nothing.

"Burger Den", he answered quickly. "I've been thinking about a *grease burger* all the way home."

Gladys picked away at her junior burger and fries while sitting closely beside her son, as he inhaled a double with cheese, a large French fry and chocolate shake. I sat across from them enjoying watching them talk, much more than my quarter pounder and coke. From time to time Jack would look across at me, wink, nod, or just smile with his eyes. Feelings, long repressed, surged through me, filling both my mind and body with longing.

~   ~

I could hardly concentrate on what Mom was saying as she sat beside me, my eyes kept finding their way across the table to where Eva sat quietly, letting us enjoy our reunion. In spite of the burger and fries, I could somehow still taste her lips. I looked down at her hand a second, and then a third time, to confirm that there was no ring on it. My heart raced.

"How's school going" I asked, immediately feeling foolish for asking.

"Okay I guess, nothing new or exciting going on in the third-grade worth talking about," she answered. "Same old, same old."

I could already see that it was going to take me a while to reacquaint myself with civilian life and become comfortable around Eva. She was the only woman with whom I had any experience, and that a lifetime ago. I felt clumsy and ill-at-ease, as though I was still in high school. For the first month I busied myself around the house fixing what needed fixing, repairing those things Dad had put off until later and never got around to.

Most of my high school friends were married or had moved away; for those still in town life had moved on and we had little in common to talk about once we had reminisced about the good old days over a few beers. Eva, I was quick to find out, had a full schedule although she worked hard to fit me in. As I thought back to the day the recruiter had interested me in a military career by promising education and job skills I could use in civilian life, I felt betrayed and angry that they seemed but empty promises now. I began to feel depressed and sorry for myself.

When Eva first suggested that I could be something more than a disabled veteran living with his mother and doing handyman work, I was incensed. I shut down, clammed up, and took her home early without giving her a response. Two days went by with me sitting brooding, waiting for her call to apologize. The call didn't come. On the third day I called her, she didn't answer. I left a message but got no return call. Looking back now, I'd call it **tough love**, but then it just fed my anger.

Ten days went by without a call, then she finally called and asked if I was up to a drive. I reluctantly agreed and was ready for an argument the moment she pulled up in her little Celica.

"Hop in," she said smiling sweetly, completely disarming me.

She drove along silently at first, then began chirping about school, just as if she thought I really cared what her third-graders were doing. I offered one and two word replies whenever she paused, thinking them appropriate without really listening to what she was saying. I guess I was sitting back waiting for a chance to attack her for the unkind things she had said at our last meeting.

I was confused when she pulled into the town's tiny airport and stopped in front of a hanger with a sign posted on the door that read **Flight Instructor Wanted**. Without speaking, Eva got out and walked toward the door, leaving me no option except to follow. I tried to whip up a case for feeling manipulated but my curiosity got the best of me as we opened the door and went inside.

"Can I help you," a young blonde woman asked from behind a counter.

"Can you tell us anything about the job?" Eva asked before I could open my mouth.

"I can't but my Dad can," she answered before asking, "aren't you my son's school teacher, Miss Sprague?"

"I am, your son is Billy Jameson," Eva replied.

The young woman smiled and as she turned to leave, and said over her shoulder, "I'll get Dad."

The door from the hanger opened and a graying man in coveralls, seated in a wheelchair, followed his daughter in. He was wiping grease from his hands on a shop towel as he held out his gnarled hand and announced, "Ben Jameson, pleased to meet you."

I took his hand as I looked into his pale blue eyes, before noting that both of his legs had been amputated above his knees.

"He nodded at them and said, "Nam."

I understood immediately what he meant and felt an instant bond, as only servicemen can.

"You are looking for a flight instructor?" I asked.

"Will you sit down and have a cup of coffee with me?" he said, without answering my question.

As we sat, Donna brought coffee and joined the three of us at a table in a little area off the hanger. Ben explained that his son, Tom, whom I had known well in high school, had joined the Air Force intending to come home and help his Dad in the business, but had been killed in combat. Tom was Donna's husband and Billy's father. He asked about my flying experience and seemed intrigued that his son and I had nearly been on parallel courses.

"Will your back allow you to fly?" he asked in a straight forward manner.

"I truly don't know," I answered. "The Navy didn't offer that as an option. I guess the only way to find out is to try it."

Both Eva and Donna were smiling when Donna said, "I'll take him up."

It turned out that Donna was a fine pilot in her own right, but with a son to raise, had no time and little interest in a full-time flying job. It took me quite a while to take what I had learned flying jets and translate it into a career teaching and flying small single and twin-engine aircraft, but I did. Four days a week I fly the mail plane and as God provides, teach students how to fly. I bought into the business and own a third of it, the other two thirds are owned by the Jameson family.

Eva and I were married in June and Mom died in December, just a few months short of having the opportunity to see her grandson, Tanner. The circle of life goes on.

Splinters From The Board

A seasoned woodworker would be the first to tell you about the hidden danger in a simple piece of wood. Wood, especially those varieties known as **hardwood**, possesses characteristics often unique to their species. Some, when milled, are toxic to the human respiratory system. Others, much like humans, are filled with tension and have the potential to twist or fly apart when that tension is relieved. We, like some boards, are filled with tension, unknowing where the outcome of our decisions may lead. I find it interesting that seemingly dissimilar things in nature share such commonalities.

~ ~

Jake, from all appearances, was just a happy-go-lucky hulk of a kid, with a quiet disposition and carefree attitude, who enjoyed his own company more than hanging out with his peers. He lived with his father and two sisters in a ramshackle old farmhouse, just outside of town. Rumor had it that his father and mother were separated because his dad drank excessively and had been abusive to her. Jake was in the sixth grade and his twin sisters, Helen and Ellen, in the second grade, but he could easily have passed for a senior high student. He always seemed dutiful

and patient, walking his sisters the 3/4 of a mile to and from school, regardless of the weather. He made sure that they were properly dressed and bundled up when the winter chill made the trip most difficult.

Bill, Jake's dad, worked graveyard at the saw mill, so was seldom seen either coming or going by the town folk. Only the drinkers among the graveyard shift who gathered at the bar on their way home knew his name. Most folks were in bed and already asleep when his shift began at midnight, and already at work when he got off at eight. Jake roused his sisters, helped them get ready, and fixed breakfast and lunch for the three of them before starting off to school. On the few days when Bill went straight home rather than stopping by Joe's Tavern he'd honk as he passed them on the road.

That was about all the interaction the family seemed to have except on weekends, when they watched Bill drink beer and watch football. Did I mention that Jake was five feet nine inches and weighed about 150, making him nearly as big as his father?

Apparently, Alice had borne the brunt of Bill's anger as long as she could before walking out one day, leaving her family behind. To most, her motive for leaving was understandable, but leaving her children was not. They had lived in Old Town for only a short time and had pretty much stayed to themselves since arriving from Oregon. Those few women who had known her at all surmised that she had probably returned to where ever she had family.

Sunday afternoon came, and with it, a variety of sports related shows and of course later in the evening, Sunday night football.

"Get me a beer," Bill yelled at Helen.

Jake started to get up to get his father a beer before being pushed back down.

"Where do you think you're goin'? I told your sister to get it," he said harshly.

Ellen, Helen's sister, cowered in the corner, tears rimming her brown eyes.

"It's time the girls started pulling their own weight, "he added. as he waited for Helen to return.

Instantly, and not for the first time, hatred blazed from Jake's eyes and a hard look came over his young face, but he said nothing. Tears running down her face, she handed her father a can of beer, before scurrying to join her sister in the corner.

Jake took his sister's hands and led them from the room and to the kitchen table. "Come on, let's get your homework done," he said softly, as he took a seat between them. Behind them, on the stove, a pot of stew was boiling noisily away. Jake turned the heat down to simmer and rejoined his sisters at the table. He looked up at the clock and calculated how many hours before Bill would leave for work.

Weekends always felt like a sentence to him, a punishment for living through the week. He missed his mother, but felt a deep sense of abandonment and resentment that she'd gone, knowing what they would have to endure at their father's hand. He'd watched helplessly growing up as his father's drinking and temper had gotten worse and worse, and the beatings had become more frequent.

Bill staggered into the room to get yet another beer and asked, "what time is dinner?" It must be half-time, Jake thought, as he watched his dad make his way to the bathroom.

"Whenever you want," he answered. "It's ready when you are."

Bill walked by, looked into the stew pot and said, "bring me a bowl and some bread and butter."

Jake stood and began filling a bowl. "We're out of bread, unless you brought some home," he said.

"What happened to it?" Bill challenged. "I just got a loaf the other day."

"That was last week and we ate it in our lunches," Jake countered. "You had baloney sandwiches and we had peanut butter and jelly all week long."

"Damn......" Bill said from the living room, letting his voice trail off.

Jake knew it would do no good to explain to his father that a loaf of bread with four people eating it wouldn't last forever. But he also knew they had nothing to eat for the next day either.

"I can walk to town and get a few things if you want," he offered, as he sat his dad's bowl of stew on the TV tray. "We are out of milk and eggs too."

Bill handed him a twenty and said, "and get me a cold pack of Bud while you are down there."

"They won't sell me beer," Jake tried to explain, before catching a dirty look. He'd already pocketed the twenty.

"Wake me at eleven," Bill told Jake, before returning to the game.

Jake knew from past experience that Bill would go to sleep in his chair before the game was over. He and his sisters finished up their stew, washed their bowls and waited until they could hear Bill begin to snore.

"Let's go shopping," he said, smiling at them.

They dressed quietly and walked the short distance to the little grocery store together.

"Hi Jake," the woman behind the counter greeted him, smiling. "You're early tonight."

Jake returned her smile and began filling their shopping cart, mentally calculating the bill as he went. He had every intention of spending the whole twenty, without attempting to buy beer.

Their total was $18.56 when the woman stopped and asked, "anything else?"

Jake turned to his sisters, smiled, and said, "Dad said we could have a treat."

They each picked out a candy bar before spending the balance on penny candy to make it $20 even. They ate the candy bar on the walk home, hiding the smaller candies in their coat pockets for later.

The girls went to their bedroom as soon as they got back, while Jake fixed lunches for all of them and put the rest of the groceries away. The television was blaring as the final quarter of the game began. Bill was still sleeping.

Ellen and Helen were asleep when he checked on them when the game was over at 9:00. Dateline had just come on, so Jake sat down and began to watch. The program laid out the details of an old murder case, where the wife had disappeared and the prime suspect was her husband. The police had every reason to believe she'd been killed, but had no evidence even proving she was dead. For the first time an idea took root in Jake's mind. What if his mother hadn't left at all, what if there had been another fight that had gotten out of hand, and Bill had killed her? Bill was snoring loudly with an empty Bud can still in his hands when Jake finally shook him.

"Wake up," Jake said loudly to his father at 10:45. "You're gonna be late for work again!"

Bill roused slowly and by 11:00 was still dressing for work, Jake had gone to bed.

The twins had awakened early and gotten dressed without argument, eaten breakfast, and seemed eager to go to school. They talked as they walked, sounding like two little birds sitting on a tree limb. He was pleased to see them seemingly happy for the first time since their mother had disappeared. What was the difference, he wondered? Had their little trip to the grocery store meant that much to them? Then he remembered when their mother had taken them shopping, always saving back enough for some small treat.

When they arrived at school, his sisters spotted friends and ran off to meet them, he however sought out the school resource officer, James Donegal. The officer smiled and greeted each student as they passed by. Jake moved close to him and asked, "can I talk with you in private?"

The young officer smiled and said, "sure, what's this all about?"

Jake swallowed hard, looked around to make sure no one could hear them, and said, "I think my mother has been murdered." Well, to say the least, he had the policeman's attention.

"I'll come and take you out of class to my office, where we can talk privately," he said.

"Can I ask what makes you think your mother has been murdered?" he questioned Jake later when they were alone.

Jake explained his mother's sudden disappearance just over a month before, the change in his father's behavior, and how they had increasingly fought before she disappeared. He also explained how in the beginning they had attended church as a family and how his father rarely drank.

Officer Donegal nodded and asked, "have you ever ridden in a police car? Maybe I can give you a ride home."

"We can't," he answered. "Dad will be home and awake by that time and wonder why you are there," he cautioned.

Officer Donegal smiled reassuringly and said, "I'll look into it and get back with you."

True to his word Donegal, although slightly tongue-in-cheek, broached the subject with the detectives back at the station, bringing a smile to their faces.

"We'll look into it," Detective Ramos said. "Does the family have any living relatives with whom she may have taken refuge? How about a boyfriend?"

"I'll find out about any relatives," Donegal answered. "You ask around town about a boyfriend. If she did, someone would be just waiting for the chance to spill the beans."

The following day at school, Donegal learned that their maternal grandparents, who still lived in John Day, Oregon were the family's only living relatives. The school records showed them as next of kin and had their contact information on file. He passed the information on to the detectives for follow-up. In the ensuing conversation, Ramos said that he had spoken with Bill's employer and had learned that up to about a month before, Bill had been an exemplary employee, always showing up on time and working hard for the entire shift.

Since then, however, he had been repeatedly late and seemed to lack energy or desire to do more than a minimal job. The word around town was that he was rapidly becoming a drunk. Interesting also, that at about the time of her disappearance, he had called in sick.

Detective Ramos made repeated calls to the grandparents without success, finally he left a message asking for a return call.

The very next day his call was returned. "Detective Ramos,

this is Darlene Smithson, I am returning your call and apologize that we were not been available to take your earlier calls. We have no cell phone and have been away from home a great deal. How can I help you?"

"Do you have a daughter named Alice?" Ramos asked, ignoring her question.

"Yes, Alice is our only child. Why, have the children been hurt?" she asked.

"Nothing like that, the children are fine. Do you happen to know where Alice is right now?" he continued.

"She's lying down resting; the chemo tires her out for two or three days. About as quick as she gets back on her feet it's time for another round," she offered, her voice filling with emotion.

"So, she's been living with you and in treatment for the past month?" Ramos clarified.

"Yes, but I don't understand what the police department has to do with any of this," Darlene said flatly.

"She's been reported as missing and we were worried for her safety," he replied.

"Reported by whom?" Darlene persisted.

"Her family," Ramos replied.

"Bill knows where she is," Darlene said, sounding irritated. "He took her to Spokane himself and put her on the plane home. We've been taking her to Portland every week for treatment."

"Oh," was all that Ramos could think to say.

Her voice softened a little when she asked, "will you ask Bill to call me, I think we have good news to share... she's gone into remission and the prognosis looks promising."

Ramos agreed, disconnected, then called Donegal and relayed the good news.

"How are we going to handle this?" Donegal asked. "Bill doesn't even now he's been under suspicion."

Ramos seemed to be pondering the question for a moment then answered, "who doesn't like pizza? You call Bill at work and tell him to call his mother-in-law and see if we can drop by tonight with pizza."

This author loves happy endings and this story has a great one. Bill called, accepted the good news with unbelief and promised to share it with his children. He related that both he and Alice believed that she was terminal and she didn't want her children to watch as she died slowly. They had argued about it but she had insisted.

Donegal, Ramos and a second detective showed up that evening with two giant pizzas, soft drinks and dessert. Three days later, the entire family drove to Spokane to pick Alice up at the airport.

Recollection

The earth seemed to be rising up toward me – too late I realized that I was falling forward toward it. I'd not felt "quite right" for several days but couldn't lay my finger on the cause. I was not dizzy exactly in the traditional sense, but felt a little shaky, as though I might be coming down with something. I dismissed the idea when the feeling subsided and no further symptoms occurred.

In hindsight, I suppose I did lose consciousness before striking the ground, but only momentarily. As I struggled to stand, both hands and one knee complained by sending signals to my brain they'd been injured. The injuries to my hands were only superficial cuts caused by the graveled driveway, my knee however, evidenced bleeding through my torn Levis. At best, I thought, an abrasion and bruising, at worst, possibly a more serious cut and or a broken bone.

There had been no one present to witness my fall, and therefore no one eager to rush me anywhere to get treatment. I hobbled into my house where I removed my pants and assessed my situation, while gingerly cleaning my wounds, before using an antibiotic cream to prevent infection. A dark bruise was already apparent on my knee, evidencing possible bleeding deeper into the tissue. When I stood, however, there was little pain and my mobility seemed unaffected.

"You're getting old," I said to myself, dismissing the event. "You need to start taking better care of yourself."

It had lasted only a spit second and what I felt is hard to describe – it was as though a silk ribbon was being pulled quickly through my brain – it felt almost like a shudder. As I said, it was hard to describe because of is brevity and because it was a previously unknown experience.

Life is filled with "firsts" which when repeated, give us knowledge and experience on which to draw, learn, and grow. Looking back, I suppose that I was experiencing possibly the first of my subsequent strokes. Aging gracefully... does aging gracefully really ever happen? I question the validity of that statement.

Everyone I have known has fought it tooth and nail, while denying the very possibility of it. In the Old Testament Joshua, who was then nearing one hundred years old, still brags at his physical prowess.

I, while not admitting that anything may be wrong, knew deep inside that something was changing, but did not seek help or medical opinion. Over the next few weeks and months, I'd occasionally feel light headed, but brushed it off as old age.

With my wife gone and our children busy with their own lives, I was left pretty much to myself. Occasionally I'd meet old friends for coffee or lunch and rehash the good old days, but by in large I gradually became a stay-at-home couch potato, only going out when it became necessary. Bad television was my only companion, it put me to sleep nearly every day in my chair.

The more I sat, the less I wanted to do, which made life seem without purpose. If it seems like I'm feeling sorry for myself, I am. I had always envisioned that I'd live until I died, and not just taper off into nothing while still breathing.

The day that I died felt much like any other in that it brought with it no excitement or purpose. I reheated a cup of coffee in the microwave and sat down at the kitchen table with the morning paper. There was little in the news that held interest for me, but it was an old habit that was hard to break.

National news was always a blend of fact and fiction these days, which forced the reader to consider what motive may be behind the author's choice of subject matter. It was a little game I played with myself, I tried to determine the truth and then who benefitted from fictionalizing it. Was it a political party, some wealthy person, or an industry? Al Gore and his ridiculous claim of global warming that had made him and others rich, with no basis in fact, comes to mind.

A ringing in my ears, followed immediately by the sound of rushing water and a blurring of my vision happened simultaneously. I fell sideways from my chair to the floor, but do not remember striking it.

"Well, finally," my wife said smiling. "You're a stubborn old coot. I've been waiting almost two years for you to get here."

Puzzled and uncertain if I was dreaming or not, I finally asked, "where am I?"

"Where do you wanna be?" she answered my question with a question.

I should mention there was nothing or no one in sight except Marlene. What I could see most closely resembled a steamed-up bathroom mirror, which allows you to see movement in the background, but not to discern forms.

"Am I dead?" I asked furtively.

"No, you are alive," she answered smiling. "You died so you could live."

"So, I died," I asked puzzled, "but didn't stay dead?"

"No one stays dead silly," she answered patiently. "Everyone dies, but then everyone lives forever."

At this point I considered if it all may be a hallucination, if maybe I was dreaming in a hospital on drugs.

"Look down" she said impatiently. "Tell me what you see.

I did as she ordered and what I saw was myself lying on my side in the kitchen of my house, waiting for someone to drop by and discover my body.

"Your caretaker will find you tonight when she comes by," she said. "She'll let the police and the kids know."

"So, I'm in heaven," I said uncertainly.

"You are," Marlene said with a smile returning to her young face, "and lucky for you, Jesus gave you extra time to make up your mind about believing in Him, rather than the good works thing you grew up with."

I was raised a Mormon, then lived my life since childhood with no religious training at all. The golden rule was my only guideline through the course of my life. It was not until my wife's funeral that I heard the Truth and learned that Jesus was the only way into heaven. I prayed that day but felt nothing and figured it didn't work or that Jesus didn't hear me.

I know differently now.

In All Probability

What's in a title, how important is it really for a title to iden-tify with the dialogue that follows, or does the title matter at all? I often choose a title to identify a particular story and as the story evolves, change it. Or, I sometimes have been given the title and the storyline follows. I have no idea how *real* authors operate. This title means to me that something is likely but not quite certain.

~ ~

She, like her peers, found herself entering puberty and jump-ing into an adult world in which she did not feel completely com-fortable. Yes, some of the other girls seemed worldlier than she, but Megan suspected it was because they had older sisters who had been through the transition, or they were acting out just for show. She was not quite sure she was ready to give up her dolls and childhood fantasies just to spend her life chasing boys and giggling endlessly for no reason. She'd turned twelve in August and just began her last year in elementary school.

Because she was a dairy farmer's daughter, she under-stood how life was created and how the young were born, which gave her a practical understanding of both life and nature. *Grounded* is the word that society uses today to describe common sense, which has become less and less common.

"Dad," Megan said one crisp fall morning, as she was helping feed the livestock before school. "How does the cow know if the bull loves her?"

Ben nearly choked holding back his laughter, finally answering, "you need to ask Mom that."

She never spoke of it to him again.

"Beth," Ben said, after they had gotten into bed and turned out the lights, "be ready when Megan asks you how the cow knows if the bull loves her, because she probably will."

"What? What are you talking about?" Beth asked, turning on the bedside light.

Ben smiled before recounting the discussion they had earlier in the day, but neglected to tell her why she would be fielding the question.

"Alright Ben, just what did you tell her?" Beth asked.

Ben smiled sheepishly and answered, "I told her to ask her mother."

"We had **the talk** a year ago when she started her periods," Beth confided, "but the subject of love never came up."

"Well, it has now," Ben answered. "I think it is good that she sees love as a part of a loving sexual relationship rather than just some enjoyable activity." He nuzzled her and moved closer as he completed his sentence.

"Stop it! Be serious for once," Beth scolded half-heartedly. "We've got to get together on this."

"I was trying...." Ben laughed, letting his voice trail off.

A week went by and then two, without Megan questioning her mother.

Finally, when Beth could stand it no longer, she called Megan into the kitchen and broached the subject. "Your Dad told me you'd asked him about bulls and cows. Do you have questions?"

Megan answered, "no" before turning and leaving the room.

Surprisingly, it was nearly two years later before the subject was brought up again. Of course, in the meantime, many changes in Megan's physical appearance had come about. She'd grown two inches, developed breasts, and adopted a more feminine walk. She no longer caught frogs with her two younger brothers or played *all-out* tackle football, but was not one to shrink away from one-on-one basketball either.

"Boys are so stupid," Megan declared to no one in particular one night as the family was eating dinner. Her brothers began to respond but their mother waved them off, waiting for her to continue, which she did not.

Several minutes went by before Beth finally asked, "how so?"

"They just are," was as far as Megan was willing to go without prodding.

"All of us?" Ben finally asked. "Or just some of us?"

"Oh Dad, I don't mean you," she smiled. "Some of the boys at school think of nothing but sex and act as if they know all about it, which they obviously do not."

Both Ben and Beth were smiling now, remembering when pimple-faced boys talked incessantly about the subject but couldn't even properly describe the parts of the anatomy. The very fact that she saw them as they were, immature teenage boys, gave them reason to believe that their daughter was indeed grounded.

Another four months went by before Megan told her parents that she'd been asked on a date. Ben looked at his wife and then at his daughter and asked her, "what do you think, are you ready?"

"I think so," she said slowly, while obviously weighing the

pros and cons in her mind. "It's just a birthday party and Tim is not like the other boys."

"His birthday?" Beth asked.

"No, it's his younger brother Tom's birthday," Meg answered. "I guess he just wants to be with someone his own age and so he asked me."

"I doubt that," her younger brother offered. "You are a **babe**."

He got **the look** from both Mom and Dad before he defended himself by saying, "well, she is." He said nothing further but his compliment did not go unnoticed by Megan either.

Saturday afternoon, under the guise of going out for ice cream, the family dropped Megan off at Tim's house. Ben and Beth walked her to the door where they were warmly greeted by his parents, and invited in. They declined the invitation but felt encouraged by it. Tim was tall, nearly as tall as his father, he looked studious behind his glasses rather than athletic, and sported an ear-to-ear smile when he saw his date arrive.

"She can stay and have dinner with us and we will bring her home," Tim's father offered, "if that is all right."

Ben nodded and thanked him.

Back at home, around the dinner table, Meg's vacant chair was like an elephant in the room. Everyone seemed to chatter about unimportant things in an attempt to fill the void left by her absence. It was very apparent that everyone in the family would miss her greatly when she graduated and went off to college, or got married.

Meg breezed in the door a little after 6:00, all smiles and with a twinkle in her eye. Her brothers teased her until she finally went to her room to escape their questions.

"**She is a babe**," Ben said, imitating his son and smiling broadly as he and Beth crawled into bed.

"She is that," Beth agreed, "We have to hope now that we have taught her well and that Jesus will guide her way."

A year later as they were doing dishes together, not in the conventional sense, Beth was emptying the dishwasher and Megan was drying and putting them away, when she spoke. "How did you know that Dad was the right one?" she asked without preamble.

Beth countered with a question of her own, while stalling for time. "Why, do you think Tim may be the right one?"

"No, not Tim, Tim's just a friend. I mean, how will I know when I meet the right guy?" she clarified.

"Your Dad was just a friend until I fell in love with him," Beth answered, remembering when she had first admitted to herself that she loved him.

"Okay then," Meg said. "If it was Tim, how would I know?"

"*In all probability*, he'll treat you differently than other boys. He'll look for ways to please you, he'll put your feelings first, he'll defend you with his life if he needs to," she answered. "You'll *see* love in his eyes and in his smile. He'll return what you give him and give you more, and you'll never be able to imagine life without him."

Beth was surprised at her own answer.

"Thanks Mom," Meg said smiling as she left the room.

Both Meg and Tim dated others through her senior year but always seemed to get back together to share the big events in their lives. They went to the Senior Prom together and afterward shared their first *real* kiss, which was then followed with a shocking admission from Tim.

"I love you. I guess I have always loved you," he whispered breathlessly.

Megan took a moment to look into his brown eyes before

responding, "I love you too."

"You looked at me oddly" he said. "Are you sure?"

"I wanted to see if your eyes told me the same thing as your mouth," she said giggling. "My mom told me I'd be able to *see* it in your eyes."

"And did you?" he asked seriously. "Could you tell that I love you."

"Oh yeah" she said, giggling again. "How about you?" What do you see?"

"I see the most beautiful loving person in the world. I see everything I'll ever need to be happy," he answered. "And... I *see* love."

They were engaged right after graduation, but waited until he completed his second year at the university before getting married on Valentine's day.

Tim eventually became a veterinarian, which was a trade in great demand in their small agricultural community. Megan, now a mother of three, became a partner in the family business.

Twelve years later she was prepared when their daughter came to her and asked, "how did you know that Dad was the right one for you?"

What is Love

Tommy, everyone called him Tommy, except when his parents were angry, then they resorted to using his full name, Thomas Edward, Edward after his father and Thomas after his maternal grandfather. Such was the way parents chose names for their children in those times. As he grew older, Tommy gravitated more toward Tom, while trying to escape what he thought was a child's name. To him, Tommy seemed too young and Thomas too old and stuffy for a teenage boy. "I'm Tom," he'd say when making a new friend, and shrink back when the teacher or one of his parents used his full name.

"Thomas, would you stand and read to the class your answer to question 6?" Miss Bell would ask, bringing snickers from his friends in the classroom.

He found that it was not as much his own age that made others choose how to address him, as it was their age in relation to his. It was the new girl in class that changed everything. She'd been seated just behind him alphabetically in American History, due to their last names.

"Thomas" she'd said as she seated herself, "I'm new to town and I was wondering if you'd have a few minutes at lunch to answer a few questions."

Her green eyes smiled at him while he struggled to answer.

That she looked beautiful and the fact that she intentionally made eye contact with him didn't help matters a bit.

"Sure," he finally answered. "I'll meet you in the cafeteria."

During his next class, the last before the lunch hour, Tom found it difficult to concentrate as he replayed their short conversation over and over in his mind. When he entered the cafeteria carrying a brown bag that contained his lunch, his eyes eagerly searched the room filled with noisy, hungry classmates. Seated alone at one end of a long table full of rowdies, he finally saw who he was looking for.

He swallowed the lump that had appeared in his throat, put on what he hoped would seem a sincere smile, and headed toward her. That he'd not paid attention when the teacher had introduced her to the class and didn't know her name immediately filled him with a new anxiety. Tom felt the trickle of sweat under his shirt making its way down his sides.

"Hi," he said sticking out his hand awkwardly toward her. "I'm Tom."

She stood and to his relief answered, "Hi Tom, I'm Claire."

God protects the young and foolish, Tom instantly thought to himself, as he worked to organize his thoughts. As he sat down across from her, he noted that her hands were crossed in front of her, but saw no lunch bag.

Without thinking he volunteered, "I wonder if you'd do me a favor. My Mom always fixes me more lunch than I can eat. Would you share mine?"

Claire started to decline his offer, then remembered what she'd heard at church, *to reject the gift is to reject the giver*.

"Maybe just a bite," she said sweetly. "I usually don't eat lunch."

Tom opened the sack and spread its contents out between

them, bowed his head and began to ask a blessing over the food. When he raised his eyes she was looking directly at him curiously.

"What?" he asked embarrassed. "Don't you bless your food?"

"I do, but many hesitate to do so in public," she answered, before changing the subject and asking, "do you drive?"

"I have my license but don't have a car" he replied. "Do you?"

"I've driven since I was a little kid," Claire answered, "but I don't have a license. I grew up on a farm and farm kids learn to drive early."

Their visit was interrupted by the bell calling them back to class.

"We didn't have much of a chance to visit," Tom volunteered as he gathered up his books. "Maybe we can talk more tomorrow at lunch."

"That'd be nice," Claire answered, with a smile returning to her face. "See you tomorrow then."

In the days that followed they met, shared lunch, and became good friends. Tom learned that both of her parents had been killed in a house fire, which had then forced her to move to town to live with her grandparents. Ironically, he knew them from church. Neither was in good health, and both walked with the aid of walkers. He'd helped them several times getting their walkers out of, or putting them away in their car.

"Gramps is going to give up driving," Claire said a week later, shaking her head sadly as they finished lunch. "I don't know how they are going to get around since Grandma doesn't drive."

"You could get a license," Tom suggested.

"I thought of that but they cannot afford the extra cost of the insurance," she answered. "We barely get by now."

"Let me talk to my folks," Tom said. "They might let me use

our car to run errands."

She engaged him with her eyes but said nothing.

The following Sunday at church, Tom could see his father having an extended conversation with George and Elaine, who from time to time looked across the room to where Tom and Claire were sitting.

On their way home, Tom asked his father what they'd been discussing.

"George has agreed to give us his old Impala with the stipulation that you will use it to drive them around whenever necessary," his father said. "It will be your responsibility to insure it and maintain it, which means you'll have to get a part-time job."

Tom was hired at the little burger joint on the corner, where he learned the ins and outs of fast food preparation and service. A month later the manager, at Tom's recommendation, hired Claire.

One night as he was driving her home, Tom asked how her parents had died. Her green eyes rimmed with tears as she recounted the story to him.

"I was sleeping over with some girl friends when it happened," she explained in a halting voice. "The firemen said that they were overcome with carbon monoxide while they slept, and never woke up. If I had been home, I would have died too."

I suppose that it never occurred to Tom or Claire to officially declare that they were a couple. Close friends already knew it and all others did not matter. Two years after they had first met and as they were making plans for graduation, Claire's grandmother died in her sleep. Six weeks later, filled with loneliness, her husband joined her in heaven.

As they left the cemetery, Tom stopped by the Quik Mart to fuel up. The 396 cubic inch engine still ran great but was a real gas hog. While he was inside paying, he saw a grey van pull up beside it, stop, and two men jumped out, pulling Claire from their car and into the van.

As Tom ran from the store he yelled over his shoulder, "call the cops, my girlfriend has just been kidnapped!"

The big block Chevy smoked her tires and soon made up the lead the van had on it. Tom stayed right on its tail as they left town and entered the freeway at well over 100 miles per hour. He knew they couldn't outrun him but had no idea what he'd do if they stopped. He knew there were at least two and probably three men in the van with Claire.

Without a cell phone, he had no way to communicate with the police or advise anyone what was happening. Five, and then ten miles passed by, until finally the van slowed a little to take an off ramp. As it did, Tom saw the side door open and Claire roll out onto the roadway and then into the gravel apron beside it.

Claire lay unmoving on the ground as the Chevy braked to a stop and Tom leaped out. Although she was breathing, she was not conscious, and he could see a rivulet of blood issuing from her left ear. He'd just carried her to the car and covered her with his coat when a police cruiser pulled up behind him.

"We've gotta go!" Tom exclaimed as he jumped into his car. "She's hurt bad!"

"Follow me," the officer said without argument, as he pulled in front and turned on his lights and siren.

Tom followed impatiently at 80 MPH, wanting to sprint ahead but reasoned that the cop knew better than he the danger the extra speed may pose. There were people waiting as they pulled into the emergency entrance. Claire was quickly whisked away inside on a gurney, with Tom following closely behind. He was not allowed to go into the operating room but was ushered instead to the front desk to provide information about Claire, before being told to take a seat.

Officer Brown took a seat beside him and asked, "can we talk? The longer we wait to find the van, the less successful we will be."

Tom nodded but kept his eyes on the security doors that led to the emergency treatment suites.

"Can you describe the van?" Brown asked

"It was a grey Ford, 70's I think. It had an Arizona plate on it," Tom replied.

The officer was writing down the information as Tom gave it. "Number?" he asked. "Did you get a look at the license number?"

Tom hesitated, trying to get a mental picture of the plate then said, "401426 I think, but I'm not sure."

"How many were inside?" Brown queried.

"Two, possibly three," he answered. "The two who took her were Latino, I think."

Tom listened as Brown keyed his shoulder mic and repeated the information he'd been given.

"Anything else?" Brown asked, smiling for the first time.

"I think they may have followed us from the cemetery," Tom said. "I saw a van parked away from the other vehicles that looked kind of out of place, it was the same color and about the same age, but I had no reason to think we were in any danger."

A squawk on the officer's shoulder mic indicated that the license plate had already gotten a hit. It had been reported as stolen in Albuquerque just three days before.

"What were you doing at the cemetery?" the officer asked quietly.

"Burying Claire's grandfather," Tom answered. "Her grandmother died a couple of months ago, and now him."

A tall, middle-aged man in green scrubs came through the doors and Tom leaped to his feet, with concern etched on his young face.

As he walked toward them, he said, "she's stable but has head trauma and internal injuries, she's in God's hands now. Are you the next of kin?"

Tom looked at the officer, considered what he'd been asked and then lied, "I'm her husband."

The doctor looked surprised as he looked at her chart, "It says here she's single."

"Sorry," Tom said remembering the old adage, *in for a penny, in for a pound*. "We just got married today, I guess I'm not used to it yet."

Again, the officer looked at Tom but said nothing until after the doctor returned to his patients.

"Shall I change my report to *married*?" he asked, smiling.

"She doesn't have anyone," Tom admitted. "Both of her parents died in a fire and now both grandparents are gone too. There's no one but me to stand up for her."

Brown nodded, then cautioned, "you need to consider as next of kin, that you may have to make life and death decisions for her... are you ready for that?" Tom could feel tears welling up in his eyes but no answer came from his lips, before Brown patted his shoulder and left the hospital.

Tom was sitting with his head in his hands struggling to focus when his parents arrived an hour later. He was unclear how they had heard about the situation and he did not ask, but was very glad for their support.

Eight hours later Tom was still sitting waiting when the doctor returned to report that Claire was still comatose and that her kidneys had shut down due to the trauma. He said that while this was common, the extent of the injuries to them may necessitate dialysis. Tom signed papers to allow them to do it should it become necessary, which it later was.

Almost a month went by before Officer Brown called to report that three illegals who were reported to be part of a sex trafficking ring had been arrested and charged with kidnapping. Claire opened her eyes for the first time later that same day. She had no recollection of the events at all, in fact she remembered nothing after leaving the cemetery. Hours later, the doctor joined them and gave them the bad news, both of her kidneys would have to be removed making her a candidate for a transplant.

"How long?" Tom asked the doctor. "How long until she can get a new kidney?"

"That depends," he answered, "it may be a week or several years before one becomes available."

"How about one of mine?" Tom asked.

"Tom, no!" Claire said immediately.

"As her husband, you have that right," the doctor answered, "but you would have to be compatible."

Claire started to object but Tom put his hand to her mouth, quieting her.

"Test me then and see if we match," Tom urged. "If we do, you could put mine in when you take hers out."

The doctor smiled at his naïvety and said, "we'll see," before leaving the room.

As soon as he was gone Claire said with concern in her voice "he thinks we are married."

"Marry me then," Tom smiled, "and make things right."

They were married right in the hospital room the next afternoon in a private ceremony, with his parents as witnesses. Rather than a honeymoon, they spent four hours in surgery and another week in recovery before returning home. May God bless their union.

The Gift

Few gifts are freely given, nearly always there is an expectation of a return on your investment, be it good will or just a simple thank you. Often, it also carries with it a sense that the recipient gives something back in return. For example, a birthday present given with the expectation that they will do the same for you on your birthday. Sometimes the giver lays out the terms of accepting the gift, "we have scrimped and saved to send you to college, we expect you to go and graduate." Or, "we bought you a car, it is up to you to insure and maintain it."

With that said, let's get to the real purpose of my writing. Regarding Jesus' sacrifice by death on the cross to allow us to receive eternal life and subsequently offering us that Gift. My question is not "is it freely given and available to all, but does it have a cost. Is it really free?" Aren't there qualifications to accepting it, beginning with repentance and acknowledgement of our sins, accepting Christ as our Lord and Master, and opening up ourselves to His will?

I, as a Christian, have no problem with this and have done so myself. I do, however, resent those who refer to it as a *free gift*. There is considerable cost for living for Christ, up to and including physical death from those hostile to Him. In the mortal world, buy one - get one free is a common ploy used to sell merchandise. A thinking buyer realizes that the free one is not free in that it requires purchasing one at full price. Two for the price of one is the same thing said differently. Jesus of course, is not in retail, He is in the business of redeeming the lost and forgiving their sins, so my above discussion is not relevant to salvation or His sacrifice for His children.

~ ~

Tom began the first grade at age six, the oldest of three children. Contrary to the times, he was from an intact home with a father and mother who were married to each other. Sounds odd doesn't it, to have the need to describe what should be the norm? Their family was one of only a handful in his class who had not been married before, thus giving the children multiple parents with visitation rights. He would not know and appreciate how special this was until much later in his life.

Tom sat in the second row, directly in front of his teacher and as such, he was often singled out to answer questions before the class. In the beginning he was embarrassed and disliked it when the teacher's eyes looked into his, he then knowing full well that she'd chosen him to answer some question. Tom was, however, intelligent and articulate and soon began to take pride in being chosen.

"Thomas," she'd say. "Please stand and tell the class what you have written as an answer to question number..."

Once he had become accustomed to the attention, he'd smile back at her before standing and reading off his answer. He was, of course, not the only one who was chosen regularly. It was soon obvious that the teacher had a mental list of those from whom she either wanted to hear or who she believed needed to be heard. In elementary school at that time, students were assigned seating alphabetically, making Benson a name that was always seated near the front of the room. Thomas Benson, actually Thomas A. Benson III if anyone had chosen to use his full legal name. Tom's grandfather and his own father were both Thomas Bensons; each however had a distinguishing initial which set them apart. Gramps was Thomas H. Benson, H as in Humphrey, and his father Thomas Ray, who had chosen to go by his middle name Ray.

Everyone except his teacher and his mother, when she was angry, called him Tom. His sister and her twin brother called him *Thom* until later on when they gained a better mastery of the English language.

"My birthday is tomorrow," Lisa said as they walked home from school together one Friday. "Would you like to come to my party?"

Lisa was a little redhead with a face filled with freckles who lived a few houses down the street from him. Tom liked her and enjoyed walking home with her, but was unsure how to answer her question.

He hesitated, returned her smile, and then answered, "I'll have to ask my Mom and Dad."

"It's at 2:00," she said over her shoulder as she turned up the sidewalk which led to her front door.

The Benson family was eating their dinner that evening when Tom said, "Lisa asked me if I could go to her birthday party tomorrow. Can I go?"

Ray looked at his wife before answering for them both, "you know we don't celebrate birthdays in our religion, son."

"But Dad..." Tom began, while looking toward his mother with tear-filled eyes.

Beth, who seldom spoke for *them* as a couple, and never argued with her husband, looked at Ray and said, "perhaps we could talk about this privately later."

Ray looked at her, said nothing and nodded.

Their family were devout **Jehovah's Witnesses** and as such, had a very rigid set of rules which they had chosen to live by. Many or most organized religions consider them a cult that had evolved from Babylon and as such not true believers in the one true God, or the Trinity. Beth had been raised Baptist and had, as a young bride, acquiesced to pressure from Ray's family to become one of them after they married, but she never quite forgot her roots, nor accepted some of their doctrine.

"Ray," she began gently and respectfully while preparing for bed, "as a part of society and our community, I wonder if it is right to not let our children interact to some small degree with their peers?"

"You should know better," Ray began. "If you open the door just a little, sin will come through it."

"But is it truly sin to celebrate the birth of our children?" she asked quietly.

"What is your point?" he replied stoically.

"I think there is room for discussion," Beth answered firmly. "I see no harm with our children enjoying *some* of the activities that their friends enjoy."

After eight years of marriage they had their first argument that night, which ultimately led them to sleeping apart for the first time.

At breakfast the family was unusually quiet. Tom was aware that his father had slept on the sofa and was therefore reluctant to bring up the subject of the party. It was when Ray left for work and Beth was busy cleaning up and caring for the twins that he found his voice.

"I can't go, can I?' he asked in a quiet voice.

"What time is the party?" Beth asked.

"Lisa said 2:00," Tom answered hopefully.

"I'll find something you can take as a gift," she answered, "but be home by three."

No one but Beth would ever know what courage it took for her to make this decision, that she knew at once would be life changing. She brooded, prayed, and questioned her decision all morning while hoping that God would send her a sign. He did not. They, of course, did not have a telephone therefore, she had no way to call her parents for counsel. She wondered if her call would have been well received anyhow since she had become more and more isolated from them after making her decision to become a *Witness*.

Tom came home from the party all smiles, excitement written all over his young face. Beth wisely cautioned him to keep the details of the event to himself, not to share it with his father or the twins, but not to lie if his father asked. Unknown to anyone but himself, it was Tom who received the real birthday *gift* and not Lisa. That gift was a small, well used, New Testament she had been given the previous year by her grandparents.

The Benson family never did recover from what Ray and his Witness family referred to as a "breach of faith," by Beth. Even though they still attended church as a family, she was visibly shunned by what she had hereto considered her family and friends. Rather than bringing her back into line with their views, that punishment had just the opposite effect. Ray moved into the guest room, leaving the children to question their strained relationship and Tom to blame himself for the rift he felt he had caused between them. It was the second week in December when Beth announced to Ray that she was taking the kids and going to visit her parents for Christmas and he could join them if he liked. Of course, believing Christmas to be a pagan holiday, he did not.

"Beth!" Ruth said, as she swept her daughter into her arms, with her husband waiting for his turn close behind her.

As Dave moved forward to take her place, Ruth scooped Tom up in her arms and exclaimed, "and you must be Thomas." Hereto her parents had never met their grandchildren. When the twins crowded forward, Ruth sat Thomas down and gathered the pair up together in her arms, while Dave did the same with Tom.

"My, you are getting big," he exclaimed to the boy, how old are you now, seven?"

"Six," he answered smiling. "I'll be seven on Christmas day."

"Just like Jesus," Dave said with excitement. "You and our Lord share the same birthday."

Tom looked puzzled but said nothing to his grandfather about not knowing who Jesus was. The **Witnesses** do not share the same understanding of the Bible as do Christians.

The visit was filled with *firsts*; their first Christmas tree, their first Christmas presents, and of course, their first Christmas eve celebration at the church. Everything would have been wonderful except for Ray's absence. The three children were full of questions about the holiday, about Jesus, and about the true meaning of Christmas, only some of which could be easily answered because of their ages.

Christmas morning was a frenzy of activity, the opening of Christmas gifts followed closely behind by the singing of happy birthday and another round of presents for Tom. They all ate birthday cake and ice cream for breakfast.

"It is all new to them," Beth explained to Ruth while helping her clean up in the kitchen. "What little they have learned from the **Witnesses** is contrary or contradicts what we Christians believe."

"Unequally yoked," Ruth answered, with raised eyebrows. "The Bible tells us not to be unequally yoked."

"But... I thought they were Christians," Beth said quietly, defensively. "I didn't know until later how different we really are."

Ruth looked directly at her, then said a little too bluntly, "why are you here?"

Beth started to cry, which of course caused Ruth to feel guilty about her tone of voice. She took her daughter in her arms and said softly, "we're glad you came."

After a tearful recount of the birthday incident and the subsequent rift it had caused, Beth looked at her mother hopelessly and said, "what can I do?"

"Look at what you have in common rather than what separates you, and pray that God will bring you together," Ruth answered. "He has promised *return to Me and I'll return to you*."

Ruth expertly seasoned the turkey and added the dressing before sliding it into the waiting oven, while Beth took out their fine china, best table cloth, and silverware to set the table.

"We'll need settings for eight," Ruth advised, "we always include someone who is in need at our table. Bert and Iris lost their home when he was laid off and have been staying at the mission until they get on their feet again," she explained. Meanwhile, Dave was in the living room with his grandchildren.

Back at their home, Ray was home from work and was overcome with loneliness. As the quiet of the evening became nearly intolerable, he found himself in his son's bedroom searching for solace. He laid down on the small bed and could smell the scent of his child before drifting off to sleep.

When he awakened later, the room was black. He turned on the small gray elephant light on the nightstand remembering clearly when Thomas had moved to his own bed, but had remained afraid of the dark. Sweet sadness enwrapped him in its arms.

Almost hidden behind the light, a small book caught his eye. Picking it up, he was surprised to find it was a worn copy of the New Testament of the Bible. Only the **New World Translation of the Holy Scriptures** was allowed in the house of the **Witnesses**, which caused him to wonder where it had come from, and if his son may be reading it.

Unknown to Ray, God's Holy Spirit was touching him, opening his heart to truth, and enabling him to consider what hereto had not been acceptable as a member of the clan. He leaned back against the pillows and began to read. When the morning's light came, he was still reading hungrily, eager to learn doctrine which he had never known.

On the other side of the state, several heads were bowed, asking God to open Ray's mind to the truth, as they sat at the Christmas table asking God's blessing on their food.

On Friday, December 27th, the telephone rang. It was Ray.

"Dave, this is Ray. I wonder if I could speak with Beth?"

Ray could not see the broad smile that had suddenly appeared on Dave's face as he answered. "Well sure Ray, I'll call her, how are you doing?"

"Fine, I guess," was Ray's curt answer.

"Here she is," Dave said jovially as he handed Beth the cell phone.

"I'm at work so I have to be quick," Ray began as he explained the phone access. "I want to be with my family," he continued. "I miss you."

"I'm not sure that is possible right now," Beth answered as she received an approving nod from her mother. "We are not ready to return home yet."

That, of course, was only a half-truth in that both she and the children were more than ready to see Ray. What caused her to hesitate was knowing that if she returned, little would change and she'd be expected to fall right back into the routine which the **Witnesses** faith would dictate.

She let her statement speak to him for a few seconds before she added, "Mom and Dad have said they'd welcome your visit, and the children and I would love it too."

There was along pause, causing Beth to consider if Ray had disconnected, but then just as she was tempted to speak, he said, "I'll talk to my boss and call you back."

As Beth explained the conversation, both Dave and Ruth smiled happily before declaring that their prayers were being answered and more prayer for his salvation was in order. Minutes, and then hours went by, before the telephone rang again the next day.

"I'm off work until the 3rd," Ray began. "I can leave right after work tonight."

"Drive safely," Beth answered, "we'll be praying for you."

The 4-hour drive took five and a half due to road conditions, but when Ray pulled into the driveway at 10:30, the lights were still on and the family was eagerly waiting for him on the front step. Never, never since Beth had married and left her home had she, Ray, and of course the children, ever spent a single day under her parents' roof. There were tears in Ray's eyes when the children ran across the snow and into his arms yelling "*Daddy, Daddy!*"

"Come on in," Dave smiled, taking Ray's hand. "We've been worried about you."

Of course, Ray did not know the double meaning which the statement held regarding salvation and assumed Dave meant the snow-covered highways.

Ray slept well into the morning Saturday before joining the family for breakfast. His children, of course, mobbed him talking non-stop about their first Christmas experience and showing him the gifts they had been given. After everyone had eaten, they adjourned to the living room where the Christmas tree was still up shining brightly, with four unopened presents still underneath.

Tom carefully chose a wrapped present from under the tree and gave it to his father, the twins did likewise. A new pair of socks was the first, a new T-shirt followed, and a ball cap was the last. Ray looked embarrassed and uncomfortable as he accepted his first ever Christmas presents, knowing he had brought nothing in return.

"Son," Ray began, looking directly at Tom. "I found your Bible."

Tom looked apprehensively at his father.

"And..." he continued, "I read it all."

There was a pregnant pause, during which everyone in the room waited for him to continue. The lines in his face seemed to disappear as he confessed, "I understand now what I never have understood before."

Everyone in the room was smiling when Dave spoke. "I think there's one more present for you under the tree," he said, before handing Ray a small beautifully wrapped gift.

Unspoken prayers filled the room while Ray pulled away the ribbon and removed the paper. It was a beautifully bound Bible, with *Thomas Ray Benson* in gold leaf letters engraved on it.

"How?" Beth mouthed the word to her father silently from

across the room.

"Your mother and I," Dave said, referring to he and Ruth as Ray's natural parents, "have saved this for you for years, waiting for this very day."

Ray held the Bible reverently, tears streaming down his cheeks, trying hard to speak, but finding himself unable. He stood as his family surrounded him, clutching him in their arms and smiling through their tears.

The following day, by God's design, was Sunday, the first day of Ray's new and eternal life.

Aging

The sun shines less brightly now, than it ever did,
It no longer seems to revolve around me, as when I was a kid.

A hundred and more friends have come and gone, leaving hardly a
trace behind,
Except now in my memory, still living in my mind.

I'll likely follow soon as well, a disappearing footprint in the sand,
Just a fading memory in the mind of man.

Warrior

His armor dented and rusted, his chain mail no longer fit,
His youth now long departed. Nothing to do but make the best of it.

He limped now as he walked, arthritis in his hips,
And hesitated often when he talked, to let his mind catch up with his
wrinkled lips.

His white hair was sparse and wispy, beneath his metal cap,
His eyes now were dim and cloudy when he tried to read a map.

The steed he once had ridden, long gone now to its resting place,
His sword dull and rusty, hung loosely at his waist.

His heart was brave and daring as it always had been,
But his decaying body could ill be trusted to support him.

Two horses pulled the wagon while he held their reins.
Bumping along over cobble stones, enduring the aches and pains.

Just one more battle, one more villain to defeat,
He thought to himself, as he bumped down the crooked street...

Our Purpose

'Tis not those things you leave behind,
the achievements and accolade that oft fill our mind.

Not the awards or the tributes on the walls,
or aging pictures that line the hallowed halls.

Not those things which man might tout,
to describe your greatness or what you were about.

While living on earth and in our season,
we question why we were chosen, for just what reason.

But finally, when our time has come,
When we march in cadence to our own drum...

To our home, our resting place,
We'll bear a smile of joy upon our face.

Seasoned by the Seasons

Slowly, slowly we evolve,
As life tests our mettle and our resolve.
We become that person our Lord sees,
When He looks down at us upon our knees.

Pause a moment from your busy life,
To thank Him now for your loving wife,.
For children also and others who,
Help shape your life and make you, you.

We stumble often and sometimes fall,
But He's there beside us through it all.
To lift us up and heal the pain,
Then send us off to start again.

– DANisms –

- The relationship you develop with your customer just prior to, and at the time of purchase, is the glue that will help you survive when you or your products eventually drop the ball; and likewise... the relationship you have with Jesus will lift you up and carry you through those times of pain and loss that are certain to someday come.

- Our God makes no idle promises and has promised we will have times of trouble to test us, but will be there beside us to give us strength.

- To expect more of others than you yourself are willing to give is foolishness.

- You cannot graciously receive until you have learned to unselfishly give.

- You cannot lead effectively until you learn to follow humbly.

- Be unwavering in your commitments, but be wise in those things to which you commit.

- While foolishness does not always lead us, it follows doggedly at our heels waiting for its chance.

- Pride, greed, and lust are the fuel for an unquenchable fire. Trust in the promise that God will provide for your every need.

- Man's law, which does not follow God's law, is not worthy of being called law.

- Be honest in all things, and especially with yourself.

- Justification is man's way of excusing what he already knows is wrong.

- Mankind's penchant for self-gratification eventually destroys even that gratification.

- Without God, what man despises most, he eventually becomes.

- Too much education is much like fine china, too good to use in everyday life, so it just sits and is seldom used.

- Life is like a cat. You can yell at it or accept it as it is, doesn't matter to the cat.

- The more I learn, the more I realize how little I already know.
- I never remember myself or my peers complaining that we were "bored." In that day, we used our imagination and brain to entertain ourselves.
- Part of winning is recognizing that it is temporary.
- Self defensiveness is the reaction to our realization that we have erred.
- Sharing a smile with you has made me a better person.
- Wisdom is often wrapped in unlikely paper.
- A major part of learning is understanding that you need to learn.
- Seldom do we know what we know, mostly we continue to search for what we thought we knew.
- Do what you do until you cannot do it anymore, then do something else.
- Make certain if you choose to take life in your own hands, they are clean.
- You'll never really know love until you give it away.
- I don't have a lot of time or a lot of friends, but I DO have a lot of time for my friends.
- Humility is not free, it costs one much to banish pride.
- Think with an open mind, walk with an open heart, and God will fill your open hands for you.
- When you become your own "favorite charity", your lust for giving will become insatiable.
- Everyone has value, some by what they teach us to be... others by what they teach us not to.

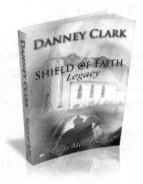

Shield of Faith *Legacy*

"One more thing, Red, then if you want I'll shoot you, okay? Thing is, if you should beat me, I go to Heaven to be with the Lord, but if I beat you, where do you suppose you'll go for all eternity? Have you thought about how long forever in Hell might be?"

Red cursed again. "You don't worry about me miner, you worry about your little family here after I shoot you!"

SHIELD OF HONOR

Amid the explosions and aerial displays that marked our nation's Independence Day, he heard a yell followed by a louder and sharper report that was closely followed by a second and third. Cady, in his blue uniform with Kevlar vest and duty belt, was lifted off his feet by the impact and fell fifteen feet from the pier into the East River.

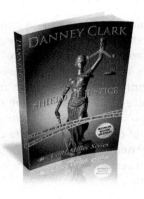

SHIELD OF JUSTICE

Unknown to others, Cady Miller was a dangerous man, having the physical and technical abilities to inflict mortal injury. His lean stature and rapidly advancing age belied his physical prowess. His pale blue eyes now retained their 20/20 vision by the use of contacts lenses, but more importantly he used that vision to see things others often missed. Skills honed through years of training and discipline allowed him to maintain an edge others frequently lost as the years caught up with them.

– AVAILABLE NOW –

Chronicles of the WIDESPOT CAFÉ

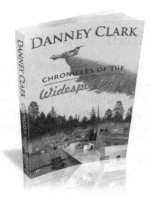

After college, nine years went by quickly, I moved from job to job, town to town, never having a close relationship or a feeling of belonging. I worked in every industry, every position, in every field garnering small success but feeling alone and empty inside.

To my credit, I lived on my earnings, not touching my investments, but spending all that I made. I drove taxi, waited tables, painted houses, sold shoes, installed computers, cooked, drove truck, did construction, or whatever came along.

Young, healthy, and able to learn quickly, I was easily employable. I have never owned a house, a car, or been married. Like King Solomon, I searched for the meaning of life, and like him, I didn't find it. I had many friends, none close, no ties, few responsibilities, felt no kinship to anyone except possibly the friend and partner I knew in college. But he had now moved on and marched to a different beat.

Then one day I stopped by the Widespot Café intending to just have a meal... that day, it all changed for me. I met Mae and Jib.

ANTIQUES & ANTIQUITIES

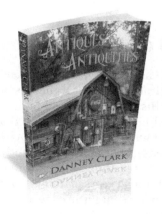

Sitting back a distance from the heavily traveled highway linking the northern and southern parts of the state stands a building which looks much like an old barn. The outside is weathered and has been added onto many times by its various owners who were not very discerning in the design.

A large collection of discarded remnants of the past adorn its mottled exterior, adding both a cluttered look and a certain charm.

If only they could talk...

These and other offerings available at the Author's website:
www.danscribepublishing.com

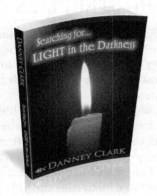
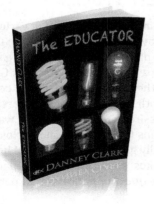

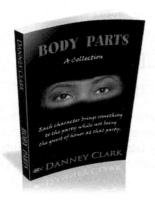

– AVAILABLE NOW –

JELLY BEANS

Within the cover of this little book are well over two dozen short stories and not unlike jelly beans, while distinctly different, they are at the same time similarly pleasing to the eye, colorful, and delicious to enjoy.

ODDS & ENDS

God's perfect plan includes memory. Memory is God's way of allowing us to relive events in our lives. We learn and grow from our mistakes, our poor choices, and take joy and inspiration from those which were right and in which we can be proud as we relive them. This collection of Odds & Ends are those things He has brought to mind and which I chose to share with my readers. Praise be to God for allowing me to share them.

These and other offerings available at the Author's website:

www.danscribepublishing.com

About the Author

Danney Clark is a third generation Idahoan, businessman, husband and father. A Christian, a family man, once an outdoorsman, hunter, and fisherman he now finds contentment in working, writing, and attempting to understand life.

Married for more than 50 years to the same Idaho-born woman and with two daughters and two granddaughters, he enjoys his life to the fullest.

Made in the USA
Middletown, DE
23 October 2020